The Book of the Claw

Also by Eric R. Asher

Keep track of Eric's new releases by receiving an email on release day. It's fast and easy to sign up for Eric's mailing list, and you'll also get an ebook copy of the subscriber exclusive anthology, *Whispers of War.*

Go here to get started: www.ericrasher.com

The Steamborn Trilogy:

Steamborn
Steamforged
Steamsworn

The Vesik Series:
(Recommended for Ages 17+)

Days Gone Bad
Wolves and the River of Stone
Winter's Demon
This Broken World
Destroyer Rising
Rattle the Bones
Witch Queen's War
Forgotten Ghosts
The Book of the Ghost
The Book of the Claw*
The Book of the Sea*
The Book of the Staff*
The Book of the Rune*

The Book of the Sails*
The Book of the Wing*
The Book of the Blade*
The Book of the Fang*
The Book of the Reaper*

The Vesik Series Box Sets

Box Set One (Books 1-3)
Box Set Two (Books 4-6)
Box Set Three (Books 7-8)
Box Set Four: The Books of the Dead Part 1 (Coming in 2020)*
Box Set Five: The Books of the Dead Part 2 (Coming in 2020)*

Mason Dixon – Monster Hunter:

Episode One
Episode Two
Episode Three

*Want to receive an email when one of Eric's books releases? Sign up for Eric's mailing list.
www.ericrasher.com

The Book of the Claw

Eric R. Asher

Edited by Laura Matheson
Cover typography by Indie Solutions by Murphy Rae
Cover design ©Phatpuppyart.com – Claudia McKinney

~

Embrace the family you choose.

~

CHAPTER ONE

THUNDER CRASHED ABOVE Hugh, the rolling boom drowning out the screech of the dark-touched vampires as they died at the hands of Camazotz. Lightning flickered behind the old god, casting him in a gory silhouette of blood and fangs. Hugh's arm throbbed with a bolt of pain that crawled across his flesh like the curve of a werewolf's jawline, though he hadn't been struck. The fires of a pack mark.

This was a place of hope, but he felt a hollowness in this battle. War had left Quindaro long ago, and while much of its history might have been lost on the shores of the Missouri River, its soul remained. The world had changed in the century since, or was it two now? It was hard to track these things as time did nothing but extend beneath the years of immortality.

Fighting was something the old wolf had experienced plenty. War. Death. These were not strangers to a werewolf who lived a handful of years, much less millennia. But here they stood once more upon hallowed ground, and the free lands, and the rivers ran red with blood.

Alan shrieked as the claws of a dark-touched found purchase in his shoulder, and Hugh was pulled from his reverie like a demon freed from bondage. The rush of pack magic surged through him, lighting his veins on fire as the fur on his distended forearms thickened, and his claws grew to the length of daggers.

Hugh barreled into the caped shadow of armor and obsidian flesh, tearing the vampire away from Alan as sure as the vampire had torn away the flesh of Alan's shoulder. Silver-black teeth snapped at Hugh from beneath the gray metal helmet. There was no conscience here in this beast, only the desire to feed, to kill.

"Get back!" Hugh barked out as Alan tried to close on them once more. One of the death bats, a child of Camazotz, surged in front of Alan.

"Hold him!" the death bat said, his voice lisping as fangs coated in the brackish blood of the dark-touched extended.

Hugh headbutted the partially exposed nose of the vampire, a satisfying crunch accompanying the loosened grip at his throat. He forced the neck of the dark-touched back, and the death bat struck. The edge of the vampire's wing, pulled taut, sliced through flesh and bone until the resistance left Hugh's claws, and the vampire collapsed onto the earth.

"Thank you." Through the gore, Hugh realized the slightly broader nose and deeper skin tone of the death bat before him belonged to Cizin. He was the vampire Camazotz had sent to infiltrate Vassili's Pit when Vassili was still in charge.

Camazotz bellowed behind them, smashing a dark-touched vampire's skull into the brick-work ruins of an old Quindaro hotel. The vampire was rent asunder beneath the grip of Camazotz, and Cizin hurried after the vampire lord.

"He hasn't transformed," Alan said. "He could have saved more of his bats."

Hugh frowned as the chaos of the battle faded around them. "I know. I am afraid he has not fully recovered from his encounter with the harbinger at Greenville."

"But he said—"

"One does not always speak truth, Alan. Not me, not you, and certainly not a vampire lord. But one should always be respectful."

Hugh nodded at the form of Camazotz striding toward them. Alan glanced over his shoulder. Whatever retort he had been about to say died on his lips.

"The battle is done," Camazotz said. "They were more organized than last time, but their lines were

ERIC R. ASHER

sparse. I suspect they are nearing the end of their resources in this area."

"You are a generous lord, and a welcome ally," Hugh said. "This battle would have cost us many more lives without you and your children."

"It still cost us too many lives," Camazotz said. "But it is not only the dark-touched who dwell here. There are darker things afoot in these woods. Are you still seeking the lost nation?"

Hugh smiled. He knew the stories, and the fictions that many in the supernatural community liked to tell about the nations of Native Americans who gathered in Quindaro, but there was much exaggeration. What might have surprised more of them was that much understatement lived in those stories. "There are few old Wyandot left in the area. It was them I sought. The remnants of the Kansas City Pack. Descendants of the Wolf clan."

"I wondered," Camazotz said, rubbing at the golden skull set in the middle of his beaded necklace. It was hard to make out the tattoo on his chest in the dim light of the woods. "I've heard Edgar refer to them as the Quindaro Pack."

Hugh offered a small smile. "They have not used that name in many years."

"Did your tattoo just glow?" Alan asked, his voice

4

still more wolf than man. "I could've sworn that just glowed red. The eyes on your tattoo." Alan stepped closer, narrowing his sunburst eyes and leaning in toward the vampire lord.

Hugh bristled for a moment, concerned how the old vampire might react to having a werewolf, still in his bulky form, so close to his chest. But he said nothing as Alan studied the circle of stone idols with the hunched man sitting in the middle, instead pulling his torn shirt to the side.

Camazotz smiled and rested his right hand on the hilt of one of the green stone daggers sheathed under his arm. The old god tended to walk around with his shirt open, but after the battle with the dark-touched, it was torn and rent, and now exposed the full-circle of his tattoo and the sleek definition of the muscle beneath the blood of his enemies. Camazotz was a force of nature, and Hugh had long ago learned to respect those old gods who were.

Zola had once told him a mad theory that the red glow was the soul of one of the hero twins Camazotz had slain in legend. Hugh had his doubts. He suspected it was more a concentration of the god's powers.

Satisfied with his studying of Camazotz's tattoo, Alan turned his attention back to Hugh. "I thought Splitlog was going to meet us here, no?"

"That was the plan," Hugh said, inspecting the bodies and dismembered vampires that littered the ground around them. Splitlog was probably smart enough to take cover when he realized there was another battle. Hugh wouldn't blame him for finding shelter elsewhere. "Wait here for a while. If he does not return, we will make our way to the old brewery."

Alan blew out a breath. "I only wish the place was still standing, and still brewed beer."

Hugh smiled and patted Alan on the shoulder as the larger werewolf slowly shifted back into his human form. The bowling-ball-like muscles of his arms smoothed into the rounded muscles of a part-time bodybuilder before his fur fell away. "You know, just once, it would be nice to have a lair that wasn't underground."

"It may be underground here, but it is sacred ground. This city once stood for freedom. Once stood for what was right in this country in a time where so very much was going wrong. It is an honor for us to spend time on these lands. Do not forget that."

"Will you shelter with us tonight?" Hugh asked as Camazotz started to turn away.

The old god shook his head. "I will return to the cave hidden by the river. Some of my children are restless, claiming they've seen things in the waters. I suspect it was merely one of the water witches, or some other creature native to these rivers, but I would prefer to be overly cautious in these times."

"Ashley and the coven were tracking a Mishupishu," Alan said.

Hugh inclined his head. "The thought had crossed my mind. It is odd that they appeared in the Mississippi, so close to the Piasa Bird's lair. Now, to find them here? That would be an odd thing, indeed. The creatures are known to stay far to the north. Monsters of the Great Lakes, it is a rare thing to see them so far south. A man of the Ojibwe Nation once told me a story of the Mishupishu here. But the hour was late, and the singing maidens floated high above us."

Alan frowned at Hugh, but the older werewolf turned away and stepped onto an overgrown path. "What does that mean?"

"It means I am doubtful Mishupishu are here in numbers, though I do not discount the idea entirely."

"I understood that part," Alan said. "What you mean by the singing maidens?"

"The stars," Hugh said. "What you know as the Pleiades? The Wyandot Nation often refers to as the seven sisters."

"I thought you were Cheyenne," Alan said.

"In a way," Hugh said, a small smile lifting the

corner of his mouth. "But I know the stories of many nations. I am afraid a great deal of what I remember are but fragments of tales that have long been forgotten." Hugh trailed off, lost in thought as he spoke so quietly that Alan could barely hear. "… dance among the leaves of the trees."

"Of course," Hugh said. "We may call upon you, if that is favorable."

"Favorable or not, we are your allies against the dark-touched. Do not hesitate."

Cizin whispered something to Camazotz as the pair walked away. Cizin turned back toward Hugh and Alan and nodded before they vanished into the shadows, trailed by the surviving death bats.

"Why doesn't Cizin look like the others?" Alan asked. "The others literally look like bats."

"Many beings throughout history have had the power of shapeshifting," Hugh said. "While Cizin may look human, or even like the humans turned vampire, he is something else, a child of Camazotz. Never doubt that his loyalties lie with his lord."

Thunder crashed in the distance, drawing Hugh's attention back to the moment. "Come. We make for the lair. With any luck, Haka will be back with barbecue."

"He's not going to be happy with you," Alan said.

"You sent him away for the best of the fighting."

Hugh harrumphed. "He is still injured, Alan. Another night and I expect his leg will be nearly normal again. Let the dark-touched who attacked him serve as a reminder we must not lower our guard."

"It's smart." Alan stepped up beside Hugh, pushing a hanging limb out of their path. "I won't argue that the boy needed some rest, but I still feel like we should be putting more time into rebuilding the River Pack. We are few, and our enemies are not."

Hugh remained silent for a time as the rain started to fall. Drops crashing against dry leaves made it hard to hear what was around them, for even a werewolf had difficulty isolating sounds in the chaos of a thunderstorm. Lightning split the sky once more, and Hugh followed the overgrown path down to a roughly paved road.

They stayed on the road until the rain reflected the lightning on the metal support beams of the ancient brewery. Hugh stopped before the structure, watching the water drip from the steel and splash against the brick and stone below. He remembered this place from other times, as if different eras now stood one on top of the other. Hugh remembered when the dark tunnel hid the slaves escaping from Missouri, and it wasn't lost on him that it was the same tunnel that led to their lair here.

Hugh walked between the fragmented pillars of the stone foundation, crowned with a blocky spire of ruined bricks. Even these ancient supports would have fallen without the intervention of steel. He stopped before the short rounded archway that led into the tunnel.

"There are not so many werewolves in the world, Alan. Thousands may seem like a grand army, but thousands can be slaughtered in one twist of fate. I am scarcely willing to turn a commoner even if it *is* their will. The life of a wolf is not an easy one, but we are fortunate not to be walking it alone."

"How long until we die out?" Alan asked. "I feel like we can still do good in this world, Hugh. Look at what we've done with the rehabilitation in parts of Saint Louis."

Hugh gave Alan a broad smile. "One is not required to be a werewolf to help those in need. You must simply extend a hand in generosity."

"It's never simple."

"In some ways, it is always simple." Hugh crouched and walked into the tunnel as lightning lit the skies behind him. Alan was right in many perspectives, Hugh knew. The River Pack was woefully small, and had been since they'd lost Carter, Maggie, and the others. But the wolves would return, those who were born into it, or, yes, those who were turned. And when those wolves arrived, the River Pack would be ready to welcome them home.

CHAPTER TWO

H UGH MADE HIS way through the low archway of old gray brick and dirt. At the end, where it looked like a wall would block any farther entry, he pushed through. The wall protested for only a moment before a crack appeared in the center, and the old tunnel gave way to a short metal staircase.

Once inside the lair—a surprisingly modern structure hidden beneath the ruins—the werewolves could stand upright once more. A massive sectional couch formed from thick leather filled the front room, not unlike the River Pack's lair on Howell Island near Saint Louis.

"Shower," Hugh said. "Haka may not be here yet, but when he returns, we will eat."

"No one's here," Alan said, frowning.

Hugh glanced toward the hall. "I am not sure if sparring with blood mages or battling dark-touched is more exhausting. Cotter and Warpole are likely resting elsewhere, as Elizabeth and Cornelius could exhaust

Hinon himself."

Alan didn't ask anything more. He headed back to one of the empty bedrooms and water rattled through the pipes a short time later. Hugh suspected the younger wolf hadn't asked anything more because the surviving Kansas City Pack members—Cotter, Warpole, and Splitlog—liked to tell some of the old stories when they gathered together. Alan had heard the name Hinon enough times to know he was a god of thunder, but Hugh doubted Alan understood the depth of that meaning.

He retired to the room he shared with Haka and started a shower of his own. One of the more exorbitant luxuries the Kansas City Pack had installed were tankless water heaters. At first Hugh thought they were a waste, but as the unending warmth stripped away the blood and grime that hadn't fallen away with his fur, he was grateful for it.

Hugh donned a set of ancient flannel pajamas. They were worn, and patched in places, but they'd been a gift from a friend a very long time ago. There weren't many physical things Hugh was attached to, but there were a handful he held on to, even if the memories of the lost didn't need them.

He looked down at the gray werewolf-claw slippers Vicky had sent him this past Christmas. Hugh had never taken to the Christian customs like some of the Wyandots had over the centuries, instead keeping with the old ways, but he held no ill will to those of the pack who didn't. Many white men called him a Pagan, as if that would somehow insult his belief system. Hugh slid his feet into the clawed slippers and padded down the hall, a small smile tugging at his lips despite the horrors he'd seen that day.

"Splitlog," Hugh said. "How are you feeling?" It had become a routine for Hugh to ask the survivors of the Kansas City Pack how they were doing. He knew how trauma could affect a werewolf. He studied the cut on Splitlog's broad nose, and the other wolf's nostrils flared. Splitlog's pale eyes squinted, and Hugh suspected he knew what the wolf was about to say.

"I can still smell the blood," Splitlog said. "You've been fighting. You should have waited for the rest of us."

"This was not a battle you needed to involve yourself in. Camazotz was with us. I know you're uneasy around the old vampire, so it worked out well that you were with Haka."

As if hearing his name pulled him from a trance, Haka started pulling various Styrofoam to-go boxes out of brown paper bags. He stacked them up on the coffee table, some of them squeaking and squealing as he pushed them toward their ultimate fate.

"Bison empanadas," Haka said, shaking the box at Hugh. "But I can't imagine you should be eating this much grease at your age."

"They're not that greasy," Hugh said. "Quite delicious."

Splitlog didn't miss the opportunity that Hugh had given him to change the topic. Instead of pursuing the Camazotz conversation, Splitlog asked, "How did you all even find out about RJ's? That restaurant is a hidden gem."

"That would be Damian," Haka said. "He has a thing for food. And if you spend any time with him at all, it'll rub off."

"And if you let him pick the restaurant, you'll usually feel it for a week," Alan said.

"Oh, I heard about that." Haka laughed. "He took you and your family to Crown Candy, didn't he? Sink you with those milkshakes?"

Alan closed his eyes and shivered. "I never knew how sick you could get from milkshakes."

Haka grinned. "Never go up against a necromancer when a milkshake drinking contest is on the line."

Alan's expression turned sour as he scraped his tongue across his teeth, obviously trying to forget some unfortunate side effects of choking down far too many milkshakes.

"The necromancer?" Splitlog asked. "Why would you tolerate such dark magic among the pack?"

Hugh popped one of the empanadas into his mouth, enjoying the flaky crust as it crumbled into the barbecue nugget of bison inside. It was a unique food, and one he would enjoy as long as they remained in Kansas City. The short distraction gone, he turned his attention back to Splitlog.

"Magicks, in my long life, have proven to be neither good nor evil. It is how they are used, and who wields them, that makes the difference. Damian has proven himself time and again, proven that he is not evil, and that he will stand with us against some of the darkest forces in this world. I've seen what he has sacrificed to save his friends, his family, and perhaps more directly to this point, complete strangers. Fear his power if you must, but he is an ally."

Splitlog took a deep breath and shook his head.

"You know his girlfriend is the queen of the water witches?" Haka asked.

"And how many of us did those witches drown?" Splitlog asked. "And you battle beside the old god Camazotz, and the death bats of South America."

"Nixie's all right," Haka said. "She's a hell of a lot more balanced than their old queen, Lewena. Of course, I do have a soft spot for her. She saved me from drowning when I was a kid."

Splitlog chewed slowly on an oversized bite of pulled pork. "You keep strange company. It was not the way of the Kansas City Pack. We were isolated, cut off from all the other supernaturals, outside of our enemies and the witch coven that lives here." Splitlog paused and frowned. "Lived here."

"At one time even the witches would have been considered mortal enemies," Hugh said. "But did you not find them to be valuable allies in the end?"

"More valuable than we were," Splitlog said. "We were allies, and they died on our watch."

"Ashley doesn't blame you for any of that," Alan said. "And the priestess lost a great many friends when that coven was destroyed by the dark-touched."

Splitlog slammed his hand against the coffee table, closed his eyes, and took a deep breath. "They were our friends too. Perhaps if we had not been so cut off, we would've understood what was coming. If we'd been able to combine our forces, things could have been different."

"You will rebuild in time," Hugh said. "It is easy to question your choices when they were made long ago. The path to healing is a journey, and you always feel the wounds suffered at the hands of your enemy, but they will diminish. And as you fill your life with new friends and new family, the scars will grow less painful."

They sat in silence. Hugh remembered those he had lost, most recently the Ghost Pack. Saying goodbye to Carter twice had been a particularly cruel twist. But Damian was still with them, and Vicky was reunited with her family. They would recover. All things in time.

CHAPTER THREE

S LEEP CAME EASIER that night. It often did after a hard battle, and there were few battles with the dark-touched that Hugh wouldn't consider hard. He stretched his back as he got dressed and headed for the kitchen. The security monitors mounted above the countertops showed a thick white fog hanging above the river.

Hugh frowned, sipped a cup of warm tea, and let out a slow breath. It might not seem like the ideal time to go hunting a monster that might or might not be lurking in the river, but there were many creatures who grew bolder in the mist and fog that twisted like smoke on the river.

Alan's footsteps sounded behind him.

"Wake Haka and Splitlog." Hugh didn't take his eyes away from the monitor. "We're going hunting this morning."

✦   ✦   ✦

"THESE HUNTS ARE fruitless, but the walk is not unwelcome," Splitlog said.

"You've lost too many pack members in the last century for all those rumors to be a coincidence. The dark-touched have not been here that long, and your brothers and sisters went missing in unusual numbers long before the war started."

"Do you think we've routed the dark-touched?" Alan ran his fingers over close-cropped hair as he glanced at Splitlog. "Like Camazotz said, their lines did seem a little thin last night."

"If you grow beyond the age of a pup," Splitlog said, "you'll see far stranger things than the dark-touched."

"Like what?" Alan asked. "I don't think we need any more problems to deal with."

Splitlog turned his attention to Hugh as they stepped over the remains of an old wall on their way to the riverbank. "I thought you'd shared our stories with your pack?"

Hugh smiled and glanced at Alan. "I did, but we have had other concerns of late."

Splitlog grunted. "Some stories should not slip your mind, especially when those stories can kill you." They made their way over the train tracks, and Splitlog paused as a train whistled in the distance.

Alan nodded. "I certainly wouldn't want to tangle with the Piasa Bird. And how can a bird that big actually fly, anyway?"

Splitlog gave the other werewolf a blank stare. "You are a shape-changing wolf, friend of a man who can raise the dead, ally of an undine who can control the seas, and yet you question how a large bird can fly? Do not die looking for the knowledge of fools."

Hugh turned to the other two wolves. "We hunt. Save your lecture for later." Hugh cupped his hands in front of his lips and gave a brief shrill whistle that reverberated as he closed and opened his palms. He frowned when only silence echoed, but it was soon joined by a sister whistle. Hugh struck off through an almost unnoticeable path in the tree line. Alan and Splitlog followed in the direction of Haka's cry.

They broke into a clearing at the river, the bank long and flat. Haka looked as if he was standing on water, though Hugh knew he stood on a shallow sandbar.

Haka raised his hand in greeting, then leaned down to the water and scooped up what looked like a long section of oddly flat rock. Only the rock unfolded, and Hugh's steps slowed.

"How old is it?" Splitlog asked. "It should be ancient."

"It's not," Haka said. "The outer layer is still pliable. I doubt it's more than a day old. Or at least the most recent layer is."

"What the hell is it?" Alan asked.

Hugh crouched down beside the stone and sniffed the air. It smelled of turpentine and sand, layered until the garment itself became as hard as rock, and almost as impenetrable. He took it from Haka's hands, letting the weight of the thing lean against his forearms. It stood nearly to his chest, which meant the creature it belonged to was massive indeed.

"Stone giants," Hugh said. "It looks old, but Haka is right, someone's been adding to it." Hugh frowned at the splash he heard in the distance. It could have been easily mistaken for a large fish breaching the surface, but Hugh had long ago learned it was best to be overly cautious.

"Out of the water," he snapped. "Everyone."

Hugh let the vest fall back into the water to slap against the sandbar. They hurried onto the shore, Hugh's heartbeat racing as he let the change come over him. As fast as he could strip out of his clothes, the fur and bulk of his werewolf form took their place.

"I am always going to be jealous of that," Alan said, stripping out of his own clothes. "What the hell did you see?"

Hugh's voice was still recognizable, taking on a faint growl as the half man half beast hunched beside him. "Something splashed in the river. But it did not move like a fish." His nostrils flared. The scent of the river was there, and the rich scent of moss and algae, the subtle stench of rotting things abandoned on the shores, and animals that hunted these waters. But there was something there that did not belong. He narrowed his sunburst eyes, studying the water so closely that he almost missed the shadow in the fog.

CHAPTER FOUR

N O MATTER HOW many battles and wars Hugh had seen in his long life, the terror of first contact never abated. In constant conflict it might grow dull, but a fresh hunt would always send that surge of adrenaline through his system, and a grim excitement for a battle he did not want to fight.

Relief warred with concentration as the dark-touched vampire pierced the fog and crashed down onto the sandbar where Haka had been standing. *It could have been worse*, Hugh thought. Dark-touched they could fight; they could get their claws into them and destroy the brain that fueled them. But the creatures out of Splitlog's tales were another story.

The dark-touched charged and Hugh braced himself for the impact, pushing Haka to the side as the boy was still undergoing his transformation into a werewolf. Alan was nearly ready, but the vampire's claws would be on him before his change was complete. No matter how fast the wolves learned to change, there would always be enemies that were a threat to their speed.

But the vampire wasn't moving quite right, a slight hesitation, almost a limp, and if Hugh didn't know better, he would have sworn the dark-touched was avoiding the water.

Splitlog was faster. With a blow that lived up to his name, he buried the head of an axe between the dark-touched's ribs. The creature screamed, and the river behind it boiled.

"Back!" Hugh snapped.

Splitlog gave one tug on the handle of his axe, but it was lodged too deep in the vampire's body, had too much suction from its innards, or the blade was caught on one of its nearly indestructible ribs. Splitlog did not forgo Hugh's warning again. He retreated, taking up a position next to Alan.

The water in the river calmed once more, and Hugh risked an attack on the dark-touched. Two savage blows and a kick to the axe handle in its chest sent the dark-touched to the ground. But it wasn't down. It wasn't dead. It opened its mouth as if it meant to scream, but instead, it spoke.

"Old wolves," the dark-touched growled, his voice deep and guttural. "You still lack the cunning to defeat us all. I've suffered harder blows from the humans, the commoners, the spider who crawls through the mud and earth around you." The vampire grunted and pulled the axe from his chest. He frowned at the blade coated in his blood before hurling it at Splitlog.

The werewolf almost missed it before effortlessly snatching the end of its handle and spinning it around his hand. Hugh suspected Splitlog was as surprised as he was to see an elite dark-touched without its drones.

"You hide behind Camazotz," the vampire said. "But he won't protect you this night."

The vampire surged forward, catching its foot on the garments of the stone giant, and the river boiled once more.

Elite dark-touched were just as durable as their mindless drones, but they were smarter, sneakier, and needed to be put down. There were few creatures in the world who Hugh held that opinion of, but the vampires fit the mold.

The dark-touched lunged at Haka, wings spreading from its back to support a short glide. It should've taken the creature two leaps to reach Haka with its limited mobility, but the unexpected assistance from its wings had it on the werewolf in the blink of an eye. Haka was no slouch in a fight. His wide jaws bit into the shoulder of the vampire, even as the dark-touched's claws ripped a hole in Haka's thigh.

"Haka!" Hugh shouted.

Splitlog cracked his axe against the forehead of the dark-touched, drawing its attention for a split second, and allowing Haka to reach one of its eyes with his claws. The black orb popped, and a viscous fluid flowed down the side of the screeching vampire's face. With its claws disengaged, Splitlog pulled the dark-touched off Haka and flung it at Hugh.

Hugh caught the beast's arm as it sailed by, spinning in a half-circle and slamming the dark-touched's mangled form into the calm waters of the river. What happened next horrified him.

The gaping maw of a serpent exploded from the river, a beast so long and thick it could have been mistaken for a dragon. Only it had no legs or wings, and moved like a viper beneath the waves. Massive fangs punctured the dark-touched, and the vampire stilled a moment later.

Hugh expected the serpent to devour the dark-touched, swallow it whole. What he did not expect was for the serpent to fling the vampire into the air, and a massive winged head to come swooping out of the mist above. He could envision what had happened, could see the dark-touched in some mad gamble to release the flying heads imprisoned beneath the cliffs, but one did not deceive those creatures and live. Hugh was not one to curse very often, but old words poured from his mouth in a language he had not spoken in some millennia. But the phrase ended with a word they could all understand.

"Run!"

The indestructible bones of the dark-touched could be heard shattering like steel in the night behind them. They reached the woods. Hugh chanced a glance back toward the river, and watched those enormous leathery wings pump to keep the head afloat. The head's long hair dripped water into the river as the maw let chunks of the vampire fall from its mouth to feed the serpent below. An electric shiver crawled through Hugh's bones as the fog swirled in the distance, and another shadow appeared. The flying head wasn't alone. The werewolves would either make it back to the brewery, to the safety of the lair, or this would be the day their long lives ended.

✦   ✦   ✦

"THOSE STORIES LOOK pretty fucking real now, don't they?" Splitlog shouted.

"How do we kill it?" Alan said, sprinting beside the older wolf.

"That's a good fucking question," Splitlog snapped. "If you figure it out, let us know. If I'm already dead, get the necromancer to wake me up so I can kill you."

"Helpful," Haka grumbled.

"It's not like I brought these things down on us," Alan shouted as one of the heads shrieked in the sky above them. Strings of wet hair fell through the trees around them, icy water dripping on their shoulders as they sprinted through the night.

"It doesn't matter," Hugh said. "They have our scent. We must run."

For a time it looked as though they might make it back to the lair before the heads caught them. But at least one of their pursuers had been far more strategic than the others, as if it knew where they were going. As the werewolves broke into the clearing that led to the ruins of the old brewery, the head was waiting for them. Hugh tried to stop, but his mass carried him forward, his claws rending deep ruts into the mud and grass as he tripped over the asphalt and sailed into the face of the flying head.

Its maw opened, and the rank stench of death and rot and decay washed over the werewolf. Hugh's senses were overwhelmed. Instincts were the only thing that got his claws to hook into the flying head's lip. Teeth snapped closed, crashing together in a clap of thunder that rivaled the storm from earlier in the night. The pain didn't feel real. He thought he'd been clear, but the head had caught his foot, and he had enough experience to know the bones were crushed. It would take time to heal from it, if the head didn't manage to catch the rest of him first.

The eyes rolled in the winged face, and Hugh kicked off of the closed teeth, wrenching his shattered foot away and snarling as half his weight landed on it, sending him toppling to the side. The head shifted for another strike, but then Haka was on it. Claws and growls and shrieks filled the night as Haka peeled away half of the creature's cheek and left a stringy, savaged mass behind. Each time he struck out at the eyes, the flying head pulled away until it finally retreated into the sky.

The other heads entered the clearing, and Alan didn't hesitate. He hurled giant stones from the collapsed ruin of the old brewery, sending them crashing into the flying head's wing. The creature hobbled through the air as the boulder fell away.

Splitlog hurled an axe that cracked the thing's skull only for it to fall away and clatter to the earth below. Haka got his arm underneath Hugh's shoulder and started dragging him into the brewery. Another one of the heads crashed into the steel beams above them, but it was too big to get closer without going around. That bought them just enough time to slide into the tunnel and escape the screams of the flying heads.

Hugh panted, cringing at the wounded foot even as his bones tried to knit themselves back together. He needed rest and meat, and he needed to figure out why in the ever-loving hell the flying heads and the serpents had appeared in Kansas City.

CHAPTER FIVE

RAPID HEALING WAS a blessing, but it didn't make the wounds hurt any less. Some werewolves were better at healing than others, as if they were preprogrammed to put themselves back together, aligning bones and fractures the same way their bodies would shift if they were undergoing the change. Hugh had always been one of the lucky ones, but sweat rolled down his face as he grimaced in pain. The strain pushed him deeper into the leather couch cushions.

Splitlog stayed nearby, frowning at the older wolf. His worry was plain to see, but as the bones shifted in Hugh's foot, he didn't have reassuring words to give. Hugh grunted in pain as bone and muscle shifted and clicked like the crack of a dozen knuckles.

"He'll be all right," Alan said. "I've seen him heal through far worse than that."

"But if the bones heal wrong…" Splitlog said.

"They won't," Alan said. "At least I've never seen them do that. Hugh has a gift for healing."

"For healing himself, anyway," Haka said before pausing. His words were hurried. "That didn't come out right."

Hugh frowned at him.

The screams of the flying heads were muted inside the lair beneath the brewery, but there was no mistaking them now. Hugh stared up at the smooth ceiling and gritted his teeth against the pain as one of the larger bones in his ankle snapped back into place. The foot looked better now, not so much mulch as just a badly bruised foot. The worst of it would be over soon, but that still left them trapped in the lair.

"What the hell are they?" Alan asked. "Hugh told us a story once, something about giants?"

"Something about giants?" Splitlog said, repeating the question slowly.

Hugh let out a slow laugh as he glanced at Alan. "I did, but some of them have been preoccupied in recent months. We have not had much peace. It is easy to let the stories slip your mind when there are more immediate threats."

Haka grunted. "They seem pretty immediate now. Hugh's told you this story before, but I'll tell you again. The heads belonged to giants who once lived in the rivers. They were no friend of the Wyandots here. Men and women would sail their canoes across the river, only to be dragged into the depths by a giant's hand. One did not survive an encounter with those monsters on the water.

"But some of the Wyandots were great hunters, and knew that if you could not slay an enemy on their own terrain, you needed only lure it to another. And so they did, and they slew the giants of the river, severing their heads to bring an end to the beasts.

"Once the bodies were dumped back in the waters, and the heads left to sink into the depths, the giants changed. Their bodies became serpents that dwell in rivers to this day, but it was the heads that grew wings and continued their hunger for the flesh of the Wyandot."

"Right," Alan said. "That's coming back to me now. And they got bigger?"

"Large enough to devour a man in one bite," Split-log said. "As you've seen."

"Okay," Alan said. "Right. What the fuck?"

"And what the hell are we going to do about those things?" Splitlog asked. "If Warpole and Marie Jeanne are going to be back anytime soon … if they walk into those things …"

"Call them," Hugh said through gritted teeth.

"Dad," Haka said. "Come on. I know you're hurt, but you can think clearer than that. We already tried.

They're not answering."

If they weren't answering, they were either dead already, or Marie Jeanne, one of the only female wolves in the Kansas City Pack, had actually talked Warpole into going to the movies. Hugh hoped it was the second option, but a sinking feeling in his gut told him it might not be.

"We can try Camazotz," Alan said.

Hugh shook his head as a crackle of pain flashed through his small toes. "It's too close to sunrise. Even if he came, should the battle draw on longer than a few minutes, he could be lost."

"I didn't think he was as sensitive to the sun is the other vampires," Alan said.

"He's not," Hugh said. "But his strength is an order of magnitude higher than the vampires we call friends. Should he lose half of his strength where the others lose three-quarters of theirs, he will be too far limited to fight something like that." He punctuated the sentence by raising his head toward the ceiling.

"Maybe it's time to bring the axe," Haka said.

Splitlog laughed. "You still believe your father's story about that? An axe that slayed a stone giant? And now it just hangs on the wall in your bedroom?"

"It's in the wall safe behind it," Haka said quietly.

Perhaps Haka was right. Perhaps it was time to

reveal that they did have a weapon of great power. Not one from the old stories, of that Hugh was sure, but one that could live up to them. But the time felt wrong. Hugh frowned, and Haka must have taken it as a dismissal.

"Alexandra then," Haka said. "Nixie said to contact her if we needed anything."

"Haka," Hugh said, his voice low and reassuring. "They're too far out. We need help now. That leaves us with the blood mages, and the coven. The blood mages'—" His jaw snapped shut as his large toe twisted and snapped. He blew out a breath and continued. "The blood mages' ties to the shadow places could awaken far darker things than what we face here." As he spoke, he pulled a phone closer. "We need the priestess." He tapped Ashley's contact, and the phone rang.

CHAPTER SIX

A SHLEY WAS IN the middle of a damn fine dream when a distant buzz sounded in her ear. She was at the beach with Elizabeth, Gwynn Ap Nudd was dead, and they no longer needed to hide what they were from the commoners.

But even as Elizabeth whispered sweet words into Ashley's ear, and her lips brushed Ashley so gently, the buzzing grew louder, more insistent, until Ashley's eyes finally flew open. There was no light in the room save for a sliver of sunrise out the corner of her window, and the bright screen of her phone. Irritation turned to concern when she saw it was Hugh.

Ashley rubbed at her face and said, "Hello?" Her voice was scratchy, but she thought she sounded fairly awake for not being awake at all.

"Ashley," Hugh said. "There's been an incident in the ruins. We're trapped in the lair, surrounded by an ancient creature, a flying head."

Clearly she wasn't very alert yet, because she could

have sworn Hugh had just said "flying head." It was one of the old creatures in the tales Splitlog liked to tell around the campfire down in the old ruins. But if things like that had ever been real, they certainly hadn't been sighted in recent history.

"Ashley?" Hugh asked.

"I'm here, I'm here. I just thought you said flying head."

"Heads," Hugh said. "Plural. There are at least three of them. We need your help."

Ashley cursed under her breath. It would figure that while Elizabeth was off with Cornelius, the wolves would get themselves into a world of shit. None of her friends seemed to have good timing when it came to asking for help.

"It's just me," Ashley said. "Elizabeth and Cornelius are almost an hour and a half away in Columbia. Unless you can wait that long for them to return?"

"I'm afraid not," Hugh said as something boomed and thundered in the background, crackling through the phone. "They can't reach us directly in the lair, but much longer and I fear they may bring the entire structure down on top of us. Even a werewolf can suffocate."

"How do I kill them?" Ashley asked. There was a time she might have asked how to chase them away, protect them if they were such rare creatures, but the days of softness had long since left the priestess.

"We're not sure if you can," Splitlog said, raising his voice far louder than he needed to for the speaker-phone. "We did injure one, and it retreated, but we did not manage to kill any of them."

Ashley grunted and swung her legs out of bed, struggling into the black leathers that let her merge into the shadows. She fastened her nine tails to the belt along with satchels for tiles and dragon scales. "We'll see about that."

"It would be appreciated if the ruins remained intact," Hugh said. "There is a great deal of history here we should preserve as best we can."

"You do like to complicate things, don't you?" Ashley asked as she tucked her phone between her shoulder and ear and started buttoning her vest. "I guess it's a good thing you had me rent this place right off 27th."

"Thank you," Hugh said. "Do not let them catch you. Their jaws are mighty, and they can devour you in a single bite."

"I remember your stories. I'll be there in ten. Don't die."

Ashley ended the call and reached for her boots. She knew the coven would be safe in the house they were staying in, but it still made her uncomfortable knowing how close her family was to the chaos unfolding in the ruins.

✦   ✦   ✦

ASHLEY WAS OUT the door of the rental property a minute later, bracing herself against the cool drizzle in the air, while she spun a tile between her fingers. At the top of the hill waited the overlook. From there she'd be able to see down the hill into the ruins of the old city of Quindaro. Most were hidden behind trees and overgrown, but the place had come to feel like a second home of late with the werewolves.

She was almost to the overlook of the Quindaro ruins when her phone buzzed. Ashley felt through her vest for the switch that would silence the phone, but then she wondered if it might be Hugh again and checked it.

The buzz she'd silenced hadn't been a call, but a text. She didn't recognize the number, but that fact slipped her mind when she read the message.

We lost Damian.

Ashley's heart pounded in her chest. Could be a wrong number, it could be a different Damian, maybe lost didn't mean *lost*. Maybe they meant something else. Her breathing came in a rapid staccato as a horrible dread settled in her stomach. Now was not the time. Now their friends needed help. She marched toward the creatures assaulting Hugh and the wolves.

She stepped under the shelter of the overlook and leaned in against the stones that framed the word Quindaro. Her focus was off. She was going to get herself killed. It didn't matter if it was a wrong number. She needed to set it straight. She'd already called the number back and raised the phone to her ear before she could think more about it.

"What happened?" Ashley blurted out soon as she heard the line pick up.

"It went bad," a voice said. "I didn't know who else to call."

"Foster?" Ashley asked. "Whose phone are you on?" He didn't answer. It didn't matter. What mattered was what he had to say. "What happened?"

The story the fairy told her cut her to the bone. They'd found out where the nukes went, where Nudd had stashed them, but the battle hadn't gone well. They'd lost allies, and in the end, Damian had lost himself. And if that wasn't madness enough, Vicky had dragged him into the Abyss with Gaia, sparing the other Fae and commoners from the wrath of the mantle.

"Fucking hell." Ashley kicked a small rock across

the ground where it bounced against a low stone wall.

"I thought you'd want to know," Foster said. "If you can help, we need it. I'll kill as many as I can. I'll bathe in the blood of Nudd's people, but I can't kill them all, Ashley. I'm not that strong."

"Maybe not, but you're that crazy," Ashley said. "Foster I don't want to hang up on you at a time like this, but Hugh and the werewolves are under attack in Kansas City. Flying heads have them trapped, and I'm afraid if I don't get there soon, they might not be getting out of this."

"Then go," Foster said.

"Are you coming?" Ashley asked.

"No, but you aren't far from Rivercene. I'll reach out to Stump see if the innkeeper can help."

"With Gaia and Damian, Foster, I don't know …" She took a deep breath. Help would be welcome, but it wouldn't arrive in time. "Aideen with you?"

"She is."

Good, that meant he wasn't alone. He was far less likely to do something idiotic if his wife was there to help him keep a level head. To say Foster could be brash was a vast understatement. People were going to die, and a hell of a lot of them. "Be safe."

"Don't die."

And with that, the line went dead.

Ashley pulled the nine tails off her belt after she stashed her phone in her vest. She muttered a string of curses as she started down the path on the other side of the overlook. It wasn't a long walk to the brewery, but it felt as though it took hours. The closer she got, the more the earth seemed to shake and the trees closed in around her. Distant lightning turned every tree branch into a fiery shadow in the dim sunrise.

CHAPTER SEVEN

A T FIRST, SHE'D mistaken them for thunder, but as she slid through the woods, quiet as she could be on the bed of leaves and twigs, she caught sight of three of the massive heads crashing against the ground. It wasn't thunder at all. It was monsters out of Splitlog's stories. Stringy hair fell down the winged heads. A wingspan that could have been mistaken for a giant bat's carried the heads into the air where they screeched and roared and crashed once more into the earth.

Hugh hadn't been exaggerating. The heads were large enough that they could easily swallow a man, or crush him in their jaws. Loose stone and bricks toppled down the rounded hill. Ashley knew the lair sat beneath that mound. She needed to act, needed to buy them time to get out, and it was time to find out how much damage she could do to a flying head.

The years she'd spent practicing with the nine tails made the weapon feel more like an extension of her arm than a foreign object. And that fact meant missing was something she rarely did.

Ashley slid to the edge of the woods, close enough to smell the stench of rot and meat left in the open too long. Of all the scents she'd encountered on the battlefield, the flying heads were particularly pungent. She flicked the tile into the air, and it sailed harmlessly toward the nearest flying head until she pulled her arm back and released the nine tails.

The whip cracked, the tile shattered, and a black cloud of death barreled forward into the creature.

The blade of the stone was a long-forgotten art. One brought back to life by a concerned friend, a power she could wield to defend herself, her coven, and her friends. The black shadow of the lightning-lit cloud crashed into the flying head. Ashley had seen the magic eat away the metal of the car, and the flesh of more than one enemy. And while it did much the same to the creature, Ashley was horrified to see the cloud dissipate and the creature flailing on the earth.

The blade of the stone scoured flesh away from its face, but even though it was wounded to the bone, it took only a moment before it was in the air once more, its attention and the rage of that dark eye drawn to her.

"Shit," she muttered, sprinting into the edge of the tree line.

But there were two more still slamming into the lair. She needed to hit them all, and then get the hell out of there.

If the darker cloud of the blade of the stone wasn't going to kill these things, she might as well try the dragon scale. Her fingers slid into the second pouch, pulling out the dark gray scale with runes etched onto either side. She dodged the nearest flying head as she entered the clearing once more, flipped the scale into the air, and cracked the nine tails forward in an overhand strike.

The razor-like nine tails met the scale near the top of its arc, and nine torrents of flame rocketed forward. As fast as it had appeared, it vanished, but in its wake was the smoking ruin of grass and scorched trees that graced the ceiling of the ruins.

Her gambit worked. She'd drawn the attention of all three heads now. She sprinted away, heading deeper into the woods, making as much noise as she could to be sure the heads stayed on her tail. Eventually, she came out of the other side, stumbled across the railroad tracks, and into the brightening sunrise.

CHAPTER EIGHT

HUGH WINCED AS he put all his weight on his healing foot. It wasn't ideal, but it was tolerable. He could push through the pain without slowing the group down, though Splitlog eyed him suspiciously, and rightfully so.

The pounding above them stopped as a frisson of power buzzed down Hugh's back. He couldn't stop the shiver. If the receding crashes of the flying head hadn't been enough of an indicator, someone was using strong magicks.

"Prepare yourselves. She's opened the way for us."

If the dark-touched had allied themselves with those old foes, it was a gamble that proved some level of desperation. The flying heads might attack the enemies of the dark-touched, but they'd devour the vampires who wandered too close just as quickly.

Hugh strode to his bedroom and frowned at the wall that held an old stone hatchet. He placed his palm against the head, and a ward flared to life, etching its way across the old blade in a sparking green light.

Splitlog liked to tell the story of Skunny Wundy, a hero who once wielded the hatchet sharpened on the tongue of a stone giant, and it seemed to give the wolf a kind of joy to say Hugh's hatchet was one and the same. But Hugh knew the man who had forged the hatchet from stone, knew the head of it was a kind of magic long lost to the smiths and makers of the world. And he doubted very much it had been the weapon of the hero Skunny Wundy.

The rough outline of a rectangle glowed in the wall, and Hugh yanked on it. The hatchet swung forward, revealing a very similar weapon behind it, only this one was gray, and had long ago been forged with the tongue of a stone giant. Hugh hesitated, pondering once more that if the flying heads and serpents were there for the hatchet, it might not be the best idea to take it out of the warded safe. But the werewolves were in danger, and Ashley was risking her life. If there was a more opportune time to wield the weapon, Hugh couldn't see it. He pulled the hatchet out of the safe with quick and careful reverence before hooking it into the leather loop on his belt.

Hugh hurried back to the front room where Haka and Splitlog had nearly completed another transformation. They'd be exhausted after this, especially

Splitlog. Rapid transformations could take it out of most wolves. He was thankful Haka had inherited some of his endurance, and Alan was as persistent as a badger.

Alan stomped toward the door, his deep black fur gleaming in the light.

With that, Alan turned and pushed the door open, and the wolves bolted down the tunnel.

✦   ✦   ✦

THE SCENT OF scorched wood and blistered dirt filled Hugh's nose as they sprinted out of the tunnel of the brewery. A few smoldering embers drifted around them, but most of the ruins were as intact as when he'd called Ashley. The flying heads had done more damage to the ground covering than anything else.

Hugh lowered his head and ran after the trail that stank of scorched flesh. Even through the rich smells of the trees and the fishy odor of the river, the scent was easy to follow. There was enough of it that he was sure Ashley had managed to damage at least one the flying heads. For if that had been a human's flesh burning, there would have been nothing left.

They crossed the railroad tracks before the scent shifted, and Hugh changed directions. One foot slipped in the mud as he hurried west through the woods. They left the tangle of vines and branches, finally breaking out of them once more and finding a sight he had not expected.

Two huge serpents waited on either side of a sandbar. Their sleek heads and shimmering scales reflected an eerie light from the late sunrise. Above them, three flying heads twirled and swooped and released their mad screeches. But who stood below them, his feet firmly planted in the sandbar as he lifted the massive stone vest and slid it over his arms, completing the garments of the stone giant, shocked Hugh the most.

A low laugh that was almost a growl escaped the giant's lips. "Truly a day for surprises."

The stone giants were supposed to be long dead. The fact there were serpents and flying heads free from their imprisonment told Hugh that some had been released, or had traveled a great distance across the lands. But those old enemies should not have been alive. These grounds had a history, light and dark crushed into one, a balance like few places had.

Twigs snapped in the denser woods behind Hugh, and he risked a glance to see what was coming. Relief flowed over him when he saw Ashley, not much worse for wear other than a few scratches across her face, likely from her own sprint through the forest.

"They brought friends," Ashley muttered.

A thud and splash drew Hugh's attention back to the river.

"You would rely on a witch?" the stone giant asked. "From the stories of the wolf, I would have thought you more noble than that."

Hugh stepped forward, putting more distance between himself and the woods, and the werewolves padded along behind him.

"She is a friend. You would do well to respect that."

"She smells like a corrupted healer. She wields dark magic."

In that, Hugh knew the stone giant was right. Ashley had been a green witch most of her life, spent enough time around herbs and potions that she carried their scent everywhere. Hugh had known many healers in many tribes, and while each was unique, distinct, there was a common thread that ran through many of them. But where that soft scent of benevolence once ran, there was a strength now, and Hugh would never call it a corruption. He gritted his teeth at the memory of why Ashley had grown away from the practices of a green witch, and taken up arms against the Fae. Taken up arms against the necromancers.

"She is none of your concern," Hugh growled.

The stone giant reached down into the waters and pulled up a club. Water cascaded off the massive old tree. It might have been waterlogged, and unwieldy, but Hugh knew one strike from that thing would likely kill any of them. The stone giants were dangerous creatures on their worst days, but at their peak they were a living nightmare.

With his other hand, the stone giant settled an enormous helmet over his head. Encased in the hardened garments, Hugh could almost mistake the stone giant for one of the Old Gods like Aeros. And he wondered if the inspiration for their armor had come from one of the stone gods, or somewhere else. But for now, it didn't matter. For now, all that mattered was getting rid of the stone giant.

"Why have you come to this place?" Hugh asked.

"Because I was called here. Because there are some things in this world of which we have no choice."

He had hoped for more of a conversation than that. But the stone giant surged forward, his long legs closing the distance between them in a few short strides. There was no blocking the log as the giant swung it. One could not block a tree. It was like standing against an avalanche, but it was not only the wolves here that would be hit. They might survive a grazing strike from the side; the priestess would not.

Hugh snatched the hatchet from his belt and dove toward the incoming log. The old hatchet crashed into the wood, but the crushing impact Hugh had braced himself for didn't come. The hatchet didn't just slice through the massive tree, it split it in two with one effortless strike. The log crumbled then crashed onto the beach, flipping end over end, narrowly missing Ashley and the other wolves. The stone giant looked at the tree in his hand, and turned his attention back to Hugh.

"You carry a hatchet."

"As sharp as it has ever been." Hugh raised the hatchet and let it fall, splitting the boulder at his feet in two. "The effect on your head would be much the same."

The giant's eyes narrowed. The creature took a step back, holding the log in his hand in a more defensive pose as he slowly backed farther away from Hugh. "The stories of the berserkers in this place … they were true?"

Hugh frowned. The berserkers were a byproduct of an old relic. A fragment of a demon who fed on fear. The fragment was placed in Quindaro when the town was still young, an act meant to sabotage the fledgling city, but it backfired spectacularly.

Something screeched in the distance, and the distant storm clouds on the opposite horizons flashed to life with a crash of lightning.

"Go in peace," Hugh said. "And do not return to this place. Or I will let this hatchet finish its job."

Even as Hugh spoke, the giant slid deeper into the river. The serpents followed, but the flying heads remained, hovering above the water.

"Are those things going to leave too?" Ashley asked.

"They will," Hugh said. "Or one of the thunders will annihilate them. And should they fail, I will pursue them myself until the last of them is imprisoned once more."

These words Hugh spoke to the flying heads, and another earsplitting screech echoed through the skies above. Hugh saw only a shadow of the thunder soaring overhead, but the flying heads saw it too. The creatures knew when they were outmatched. The heads turned, and floated deeper into the mist until they became nothing but shadows.

CHAPTER NINE

"I NEED TO sleep," Haka said. "A lot. And deeply."

Hugh inclined his head. "We all need rest."

"Are you sure those things are gone?" Alan asked.

"For now," Hugh said.

"The stone giants are not as stupid as some would like to think," Splitlog said. "Even they can learn, though they may need to be reminded from time to time of what they learned."

Hugh turned to Ashley. "Thank you, Priestess. Your assistance is always welcome."

"It's the least I can do," Ashley said.

"Chasing off flying heads is the least you can do?" Alan said. "I think there's far less you could have done."

Ashley gave him a small smile, looking the werewolf up and down, before wringing her hands together. "I have news. Have you heard about Falias?"

"Nothing since Nudd's ... presentation," Hugh said, the words tasting foul on his tongue.

Ashley nodded. "It got worse. We … we lost Damian. Foster called me."

The hollowness in the pack magic, the bolts of pain Hugh had felt in his arm … he'd suspected as much. It's where he'd marked Damian as pack. Ashley's phone buzzed and she slid it out of her vest. "It's Elizabeth. She's heading back."

He watched as Ashley's fingers trembled across the front of the phone. She wiped her eyes and angrily pecked out a message back to Elizabeth.

"Are you okay?" Hugh asked.

Ashley shook her head. "I will be. It's just … He's always been a friend of the coven. Him and Zola both, and the fairies. We already lost Cara …" She trailed off, her lips trembling. "We've already lost so many."

"Vicky and Sam?" Hugh asked, feeling a weight settle in his chest.

"They're alive," Ashley said. She took a deep breath. "It's the only good news Foster had. They got Gaia to drag him into the Abyss somehow. I don't know any more than that."

A cool anger rose in Hugh, different than the fury he knew in his wolf form. It was an odd sensation, and one he had not felt in some time. There was the raw rage of battle, and the anger one felt engaging their enemies, but this was different. This was a cold and calculating thing, and Ashley's words reminded him of the betrayals of the Fae.

It did not take long for him to realize what had happened. Hugh looked at Splitlog and said, "The Heart has awakened."

"Are you sure?" Splitlog asked.

"I am," Hugh said. "Can you not feel it, the anger, but the rational edge that holds it in check? The fear, tempered by the knowledge of what must be done." Hugh shook his head. "The flying heads, the stone giants, the serpents. Even the Piasa Bird has shown itself. Everything is returning to Quindaro because its Heart has awakened."

"They're here to take it," Splitlog said, his voice almost a growl. "We have to stop them."

"I'm pretty sure we already did," Haka said. "They ran that way." He pointed to the river.

Hugh frowned. "He'll be back. If we're lucky, won't be until nightfall, when Camazotz can aid us in earnest. But I am not willing to trust things to luck this day. Come, we make for the Heart."

Ashley stepped up behind Hugh as they started back toward the woods. She brushed against his arm and for a moment, wrapped her fingers around his wrist, squeezed, and let go. Hugh embraced her with one arm, knowing there was nothing he could say to

57

make the danger her friends were in any less. But he could be here for her, to support the coven, and save those who were under threat of the machinations set in motion by Gwynn Ap Nudd.

"What is the Heart?" Ashley asked.

"An old relic, a dangerous one too, but if the Heart of Quindaro has awakened, the time may be here that it is needed once more," Splitlog said. He told her the story of the demon that was slain and imprisoned, only to have its very essence used as a weapon. Told her how that weapon was twisted, and brought those who would have been enemies together against a common foe, forming the Heart of the city that was far ahead of its time.

There were some stories about the Heart that it was not Hugh's place to tell. But there were some of their friends who needed to hear.

Hugh led them single file through one of the overgrown paths, headed for the ruins of the stone cabin, one of the few residential buildings whose ghost still survived in old Quindaro.

"Zola and Philip spent time in Quindaro." Hugh glanced back at Ashley. "Did you know?"

"No."

"Seriously?" Alan asked.

Hugh nodded. "Quindaro was a stop, one might

say a stronghold, for the Underground Railroad during the Civil War. Many men and women found their way here, though not all survived."

"The Signal Tree in the graveyard," Ashley said. "Slave catchers?"

"Catchers," Hugh said, letting the word trail off. "They were murderers. Those who did not evade them as they crossed the river died. Some of them are buried in the old cemeteries, some in unmarked graves. They almost caught Zola. I suppose you could say they did catch Zola, much as a man catches a rockslide."

"Good fucking riddance," Alan growled.

Hugh nodded. "Zola spent time here. And the Heart was one of the things that helped break through her rage. Her bias against all men who could be a threat."

"So the Heart was what, like a therapist?"

Hugh chuckled. "Not in the slightest. You see, in this place, our nations and white men and freedmen worked together. Not only for the greater good, but simply to be good. United against common enemies, friendships thrived while at the same time the prejudices of thousands of people died away."

"There are always prejudices among the commoners," Splitlog said. "That will never change."

"It can change," Hugh said. "It may never leave

entirely, but it can change, and people can be better for it. And that my friends is what the Heart did."

✦   ✦   ✦

THE SUN ROSE higher into the sky as they reached the overgrown ruins of the stone cabin. There were few people left alive who knew what the Heart of Quindaro was, and even fewer who knew where it was hidden. So when they crossed the threshold of the stone cabin, Hugh froze when he realized it was not a shadow across from them, but a Fae dressed in obsidian armor.

Hugh's arm flashed out to the side, bringing his allies to a halt. The surprise was apparently not his alone, because the Fae slowly folded his arms and took a step back himself. "I thought this place was abandoned."

"Mostly," Hugh said.

"Who is that?" Ashley hissed. Her hand flexed against the coil of the nine tails at her belt, its leather creaking.

Hugh gave her a tiny shake of his head, and she stilled.

"What brings a knight of the Unseelie Court to Kansas City?" Hugh asked.

He thought it best not to play dumb, but the stiffening backs of Alan and Ashley told him they hadn't had a clue this Fae was Unseelie.

"Kansas City, you say," the Fae said, slowly nodding his head. "And here I thought this was called Quindaro."

Hugh narrowed his eyes. "My words were not meant to deceive you. We are quite literally within the limits of what they call Kansas City."

"I am aware, wolf," the Fae said.

Hugh studied the intricate lines etched in the fairy's armor. There wasn't much he recognized until the Fae turned slightly, and a circle of spires was plain to see on the Fae's shoulder. Murias. He'd not known many Fae who had kind words to speak about the old fairy city.

The Fae lifted his helmet and tucked it beneath his arm, revealing a grayish skin that almost looked like the dead. Shadows flexed behind the fairy, and it took Hugh a moment before he realized part of the fairy's wings were translucent. Only the scarcest edge of an outline even betrayed the fact that they were there.

The fairy took a deep breath, and a small smile curled the edges of his lips. Hugh had seen the expression on the faces of a hundred men. It was a promise of violence, the hatred of generations. And the words that came out of the fairy's mouth surprised him not. "This will not end well for you."

"There is no need for conflict this day," Hugh said,

keeping his voice even and calm. "Be on your way. Go in peace and my people will not strike at you."

The fairy slid his helmet back on, the scorched black of his eyes almost vanishing in the shadows. "Peacemakers. Your way is folly, but I am not without generosity. Your death will be swift." The Fae raised two fingers, and the woods around them exploded into fury.

CHAPTER TEN

"Y OU RISK MUCH, asking favors of Murias once more," the dark-touched vampire sitting in the corner said, drawing Nudd's eye.

Nudd's pacing slowed, and he studied the figure for a moment. Without its helmet on, he could almost see the similarities to the fairies of Murias, the gray skin and pitch black eyes, though the dark-touched were different. Some scholars suspected they were half Unseelie and half Eldritch. Nudd always thought they looked too humanoid for that. But their strength was uncanny, and perhaps there was something to the rumor.

"My debt to Murias will be paid," Nudd growled, failing to hide his anger entirely. "Your masters will be compensated as agreed."

The dark-touched smiled, revealing a glint of its fangs. "You've already lost your weapon. How many years, decades, *centuries*..." The dark-touched drew out the word. "How long have you been plotting, only to fail again? Your obsession with the sons of Anubis has led you nowhere. You cannot mask that fact from my masters. And given that, they have withdrawn much of our forces."

"I did not fail," Nudd snapped. "Given time, those fools will try to save Vesik. If they mean to save him, they'll have to bring him back to this realm. And then I will reclaim my prize."

"Then why send soldiers to Quindaro? Your logic fails. It is not in pursuit of our goal. It is clear you are lost, and your promise to us has gone unfulfilled. We seek a better path."

Nudd looked away, the flexing of his jaw hidden from the vampire. He didn't want the dark-touched to abandon their alliance, but he could see their perspective. See how they thought he'd already failed. As if the fools believed Damian was his only card to play.

"Vesik's allies are predictable. Even if they believe Damian to be lost, they won't be willing to sacrifice his sister, or the child. And you know what ties those three together? You understand what our spies uncovered about them?"

The dark-touched looked like it was about to speak, but Nudd cut it off.

"A blood knot. A blood knot ties those souls together, and the death of one means the death of all three. That's why they're off-limits. There are few things in this world that can change the anchor of the blood knot. One of those pieces lies in Quindaro. That is why our soldiers are there. Once enough of his allies are slain, we can move forward with the rest of the plan."

"Your limits do not affect us, Nudd. Your word has been broken." The dark-touched slowly crossed its arms and eyed Nudd in the torchlight. "And what if they prove more resilient than you know? The price will still be due."

Fury rose in Nudd's chest. Rage was something he'd spent centuries learning to master, but to be questioned by this maggot, an informant he knew would take word back to the members of his failing alliance, that he had no need to abide.

Nudd didn't share his thoughts with the vampire. Instead, he closed his eyes and felt for the threads of magic stretched out across the country, holding the devils at bay. And with a simple tug, an unraveled ley line, the gateways ripped open. In short order, the Eldritch things of old would leave his enemies with no room to maneuver.

And if the dark-touched become an obstacle in their foolish retreat, they'd meet their end in the same blow.

CHAPTER ELEVEN

S OMETIMES WHEN THINGS went wrong, it was easy enough to overcome them. But Hugh reflected on the fact that lately it seemed when anything went wrong, they were presented with a nearly insurmountable obstacle or threat. This was no different.

Hugh worried about his allies in these conflicts, especially those not gifted with healing, but Haka wasn't one of them. Carter had once asked Hugh why he wasn't more concerned about Haka when it came to some of their more violent conflicts. The answer was simple: Haka's prowess was nearly the equal of any wolf.

Haka sprang forward, whatever exhaustion he'd felt from two changes in the clash with the flying heads forgotten. Dark fur that would have vanished in the shadows of the night gave off a rich auburn sheen as Haka wove through the Unseelie Fae.

Fighting the Unseelie was a different beast than fighting Nudd's regular Fae. The Knights of the Seelie

Court fought in a relatively straightforward fashion. Hugh might need to worry about a hidden blade or a stealthy spell, but the Unseelie Fae were deception incarnate, a fact Splitlog learned with some pain.

One of the Fae dove at Haka as if to impale him on a glowing blade, only to shift at the last moment as Splitlog tried to close the gap, instead taking the full length of the blade through the meat of his bicep. The werewolf howled as the magic seeped into his body.

Hugh had been struck by a blade like that before, and where the magic of the Seelie Fae was warmth, fire, and flame, the Unseelie were cold icy death. Harder to heal, but still possible. Hugh surged into action, from one step to the next, his form shifting, magic rippling through his muscles until it was not the man closing on the Unseelie Fae, but the old wolf with a hatchet grasped in his claws.

Another Fae scored a glancing blow against Haka, singeing fur and flesh, but it left him open, and the crack of Ashley's nine tails sent a spear of nothingness rocketing through the fairy's chest. The Fae collapsed without so much as a look of surprise on his face before his body erupted into a cloud of ashen glitter, the screams of his dissolution echoing as he vanished into the ley lines.

The Fae who had impaled Splitlog abandoned his

sword to the werewolf's arm and pulled another blade as he turned to face Hugh. The fairy raised a shield to block the blow from the hatchet. The old blade split the shield and severed the arm behind it. The fairy screamed, but even as he tried to backpedal, his wings going wide, Hugh's claws found the fairy's throat and silenced the Unseelie Fae.

Even as cartilage and bone gave a satisfying crunch beneath his grasp, Hugh felt fire erupt in his left thigh. Pain blistered across his nerve endings and his flesh grew cold before he ripped the enchanted arrow from his leg. Still the pain lingered, the muscle compromised, and he barely caught the flicker of blue light in the trees above them before the next arrow found its mark.

Alan grunted as blue fire licked at his black fur, but it didn't stop the massive wolf. Alan continued to slowly and deliberately climb the tree. Apparently realizing it had miscalculated, the Unseelie Fae launched into the air, only to have his ankles snatched by Alan's claws, and his inertia turned toward the ground as he slammed into one of his allies.

The first Fae backed toward the edge of the stone cabin's ruins. "That is quite enough." The Fae let out a humorless laugh, and a cold blue light came into life before it, expanding outward faster than Hugh could react. It hit like a cannon shot, hurling him backward into stones and sending him toppling over the side of the cabin ruins. A tree trunk shattered where Alan crashed through it, and another groaned as Haka bounced off it. But even as Hugh climbed back to his feet, he saw Ashley, rising from the shelter she'd taken behind the low-lying wall of the stone cabin and flicking a dragon scale into the air. The nine tails cracked and a spinning disc of bright blue flame erupted across his field of vision, cutting through one of the fairies in the canopy, and sending the tops of several trees crashing to the earth with the screams of the Fae.

The speaker flicked his wrist, and Ashley grunted, stumbling backward a step before falling down, clutching her chest. Hugh heard her curse, and he hoped that meant the wound was not mortal.

"You've grown soft, high-backed wolf. You don't remember me, but I remember you. You attack us as if we were brainless dark-touched vampires. Your people have paid the price. Now surrender the Heart or die."

But Hugh didn't have words for the Unseelie Fae. He was too busy backpedaling, drawing away from the fairy, and the Fae released a triumphant laugh.

Hugh scooped up Ashley, blood staining her fingers, before he looked over his shoulder one more time and bellowed, "Run!"

The light of a portal opened in earnest, and through that sickly red gateway poured the tentacles of a leviathan.

CHAPTER TWELVE

THEY'D BEEN INJURED. Badly. It had only been six or seven of the Unseelie Fae waiting to ambush them, but it had been enough. They were in trouble, and the irony of the massive leviathan pouring through that portal and crushing three of them beneath its maw was not lost on Hugh.

"Was that a leviathan?" Splitlog asked. "I've heard of them, but to see one … by the gods."

"Your leg," Haka said, studying Hugh as he limped, crashing through the woods.

"No time for that now," Hugh said. "We can't run from this. That thing is too close to the Heart. We can't risk it falling into Nudd's hands."

"Or those Unseelie bastards," Ashley grumbled. "This fucking hurts."

"I'm afraid they're on the same side," Hugh said.

"Are you kidding?" Alan asked. "That leviathan was gobbling up fairies like they were cheese balls."

"Nudd does not value the lives of his people," Hugh

said.

"I don't think they *are* his people," Haka said. "For all Nudd might admire the Unseelie courts, he's not one of them. He's a bastard, and a murderer, but he's not Unseelie."

Hugh grunted and gently laid Ashley down. He prodded the wound, relieved to see the blade was at an odd angle and had most likely missed her lung. Pulling it out would still be dangerous. "We need a healer."

"Well, there were a bunch of fairies back there," Ashley said, her voice taking on an almost violent edge. "Maybe one of them will help."

Hugh gave her a tight smile. He pulled out his phone, frowning in frustration as his clawed fingers tried to work the screen. He finally managed to unlock it and tapped the innkeeper's contact. She picked up after two rings.

"I wasn't expecting to hear from you so soon," the innkeeper said.

"So soon?" Hugh asked.

"Are Vicky and Luna already there?"

"No, but that's not why I'm calling. Why are they...? It doesn't matter now. We have Unseelie Fae in Quindaro, and there's a leviathan here that came through a portal."

"What the hell are you talking to me for? Go kill it."

"They ambushed us," Hugh said, his voice taking on an edge of strain that it rarely showed. "Ashley's been hurt, and we need a healer. Can you find someone? Quickly?"

"Oh my God, you people are going to kill me," the innkeeper said. She kept muttering something that Hugh couldn't make out as the line went dead.

"I think help's on the way," Hugh said. "In the meantime, we need to get the Heart."

He stared down at Ashley before looking back toward the path that would lead them to the leviathan and the Unseelie Fae once more. "One of us needs to stay behind with Ashley."

But before Hugh could speak another word, Ashley snapped, "Like fucking hell they do."

"I will," Haka said.

"No, you won't," Ashley said. "I'm not helpless here, and I'm not dead yet. The innkeeper has a healer on the way…" Ashley grimaced and clutched at her side. "I'll wait here for the healer. You need all the help you can get with the leviathan. Now go, before it finishes off the Unseelie and heads somewhere else."

Hugh had always preferred strategy to passion. To be passionate in a dire situation would often lead to the death of friends and allies. But given enough time to plan, Hugh could be a devastating tactician, applying the strengths and weaknesses of his allies where they'd be most effective. And though here, now, they didn't have time to plan carefully, he was sure of a few things.

The innkeeper would be true to her word, and whether or not any of them stayed with Ashley likely wouldn't have an impact on her survival. Splitlog knew the territory better than anyone else in the group. That might not have been the case if it was still the heyday of Quindaro, but it wasn't.

Alan and Haka would be his tanks here. They were both angry, restless, and whether they encountered a group of Unseelie Fae, or the massive tentacles of the leviathan, their enemy would not fare well. But any scenario he pictured that he dragged Ashley with them did not end well. The only choice was to leave her here. She might have made that decision in the blink of an eye, but he needed a minute to ponder the situation. In the end, he knew she was right.

Hugh nodded. "Send up flames if you need our help, and we'll return as soon as we can. You can still crack that whip?"

"I don't know if I'm supposed to make a Triwizard joke or a Devo joke," she said through gritted teeth. "I won't need the whip since I don't mind singeing my fingers a bit."

"Probably for the best," Hugh said. "Be careful with

that blade in your chest. I think it missed your lung, but if it's plugging any damage to your arteries, you could bleed out in minutes."

Ashley used her legs to push herself deeper into the loam of the forest floor. "Get out of here."

Hugh nodded and gathered up the werewolves. They started back toward the ruins of the stone cabin.

CHAPTER THIRTEEN

"YOU FOUGHT ONE of those things before?" Splitlog asked.

Hugh nodded. "The three of us have, yes."

"And you know how to defeat them?" Splitlog asked, a small edge of hope in his words.

"Yes," Hugh said after a moment of hesitation.

"And have you ever defeated one?"

"Not on our own," Alan said.

"Wonderful," Splitlog grumbled. "What do you know about these things?"

"They have three beaks," Hugh said. "Stay away from them, or you likely won't heal from it."

"Won't heal?" Splitlog asked.

"Because you'll be mulch," Alan said.

Hugh rubbed his thumb over the head of the axe head on his belt. "We have better weapons for this encounter. You can attack the tentacles, you can even tear them off, but they will regenerate given enough hours, or days. You must kill it. Its only real weakness is its eyes."

"And they're damn hard to get to," Alan said. "So you think if we can get you into the eye, that hatchet will do the rest?"

"It must."

"How many eyes does it have?" Splitlog asked. "Should we approach multiple sides for the best chance of getting through?"

Hugh nodded. "But that's not the best defense if we run into more Unseelie Fae. It would be better to stay together to fight off the Fae, but best to divide our forces to battle the leviathan. We face a risk either way."

"I can kill the Unseelie on my own easier than all of us getting pancaked at once by the leviathan," Haka said.

"I agree," Hugh said. "But that doesn't mean the Fae are less dangerous. The eyes are on either side of the beaks. Pierce them."

Splitlog shook his head. "This is insane." He hesitated and then said, "I'll come from the South. Alan, you're the fastest of all of us. Why don't you go north and circle around to attack the leviathan from behind. Haka and Hugh, you can flank from the other sides."

There were many alpha wolves who would've taken umbrage with Splitlog giving orders to members of their own pack. But Hugh had always been different in that regard. He was patient where most wolves were brash, and able to focus his anger where it would be most effective, like selecting a tool for the job it was best built for. Splitlog was an old war dog himself. A good mind for strategy, with knowledge of the local land, and someone Hugh trusted in full with his life and Haka's.

Alan looked to Hugh, and Hugh only nodded as if silently giving him permission to do whatever Splitlog suggested.

The wolves didn't need more instruction than that. Part of that was the pack bond, and part of that was being friends for so long. And even as Hugh thought of the pack bonds, his arm flooded with power, the nerves tingled where he could usually sense Damian, but it was different, darker, and a fiery kind of electricity.

The wolves separated, and Splitlog vanished into the tree line. Hugh stayed on the relatively clear path that would take him directly back to the stone cabin even as Haka and Alan sprinted to the north. There were only a few times in history where Hugh had witnessed a world-changing event. But these days, in the darkness brought forward by Gwynn Ap Nudd, it felt very much like a time that had weight. As if things that had been in motion for an eternity were finally reaching their end.

He'd seen it happen, when the white men brought their genocide to the nations of the plains, and the centuries of war that followed. Fools who murdered and razed the land so they could drown it in the pollution of their own unbridled ambition. And the warmongers did what they do best after the wars ended here. They spread, until Europe and Asia were covered in a sea of corpses. Nudd's actions felt familiar, great swaths of the world coming together to fight a common enemy, while their enemies did the same. Hugh feared the footsteps of the Mad King would leave a ruin to rival the worst of mankind.

✦　　✦　　✦

THE CRIES OF the Unseelie Fae grew louder as Hugh closed on the ruins of the stone cabin. Splitlog had vanished into the trees, and Hugh could not hear so much as the whisper of the old wolf's steps in the underbrush. He could track Haka and Alan for a time, Alan being far less experienced in the wilderness, but even the distant whispers of their footsteps were lost to the cries of battle and the earthshaking impact of the leviathan's tentacles.

The leviathan's limbs rose higher than the tree line. Fleshy gray tentacles, thick as tree trunks, whipped through the air, breaking saplings and Fae and old oak trees alike. It was the kind of thing that could kill even the best healers. It was possible for a werewolf to be crushed, smashed, and cut apart faster than their abilities could heal them. Hugh had seen it done. Had seen it happen in wars and, worse, he'd seen it happen methodically as executions.

One of the Unseelie Fae stood just on the opposite side of the wall as Hugh hurdled it. He met the eyes of the fairy, wide black pupils with only the tiniest hint of a dark gray iris. Hugh raised his hatchet, ready to strike down the Fae, but the fairy didn't react, he only turned back to the leviathan, sword held loosely in his hand.

Hugh growled and spun the hatchet of stone. "Fight or die."

The fairy staggered as Hugh shoved him away, barely catching himself on the edge of the wall before dodging a collapsing tree. Hugh thought the fairy must've been young to show that much shock in the presence of his enemy. But the leviathan was an imposing form, and he could understand how if one was not ready to look into the face of madness, one might not return. Hugh thought the fairy might be the smartest of them when his wings flexed and vanished through the forest canopy.

As fast as the leviathan smashed one tree trunk to

the ground, the tentacle shifted, lashing out across the width of the stone cabin until it crashed into the remnants of a brick wall. Boulders hurtled through the air at the impact. The whiplash was unthinkably quick. A smaller tentacle snapped like a bullwhip, displacing air and smoke as the fires of a Fae incantation swelled around it.

A sound like a gunshot echoed through the woods as the tentacle unfurled and reached the end of its length. Hugh vaulted onto the rubbery gray flesh, claws digging in, careful to avoid the hooks inside of those giant suction cups. He bounced from one tentacle to the next, using his claws to lever his way up, farther into the ball of wildly flailing flesh.

In his many years, he'd told more than one wolf that fighting a leviathan was a stupid way to die. And yet here he was, burying himself deeper in the knot of rancid flesh, roaring as a tentacle grazed his thigh, and the hooks latched on, dragging him closer, until at last he could see the first of the mighty beaks within. It almost looked like the beak of a giant parrot, with rows of saw-like teeth waiting inside. Hugh would have been more comfortable sticking his arm down the throat of a shark.

What was left of the Unseelie fairies continued fighting. This was not an enemy they'd expected to face. Hugh only saw glimpses of two or three of the Fae who were still alive, and there was more than one set of armor strewn across the ground, smashed flat by the leviathan, or sawed into bits by mighty beaks. Hugh could be as fast as lightning, but once a leviathan had you, it had you.

He waited until the tentacle started to curl back onto itself. Timing it wrong would mean his death. Timing it right might not be better.

Hugh was close enough to move when he heard Haka cry out. His focus cracked, the angle of his strike lost as he turned, frantically trying to find the cries of his son.

Near the ground, beneath the edge of a savaged tentacle, Haka was down on one knee, the arrow of an Unseelie Fae pulsing with blue light in his leg.

Hugh cursed and brought the hatchet down, slicing deeply into the thick tentacle that had him by the thigh. His timing was rotten, and he knew it, but he had to get to Haka. He caught a glimpse of Haka grunting and scratching as one of the tentacles spiraled its way around his chest, locking one of his arms against his side until the wolf was far less of a threat.

A barrage of fiery arrows pierced the night from the other side of the stone cabin as Splitlog joined the fight. Two found their mark in the thick flesh around

THE BOOK OF THE CLAW

the leviathan's beaks, and even in that damp gray rubber, the flames still burned. It was an old trick, one he'd often heard called Greek fire. But more than anything it reminded him of napalm.

Hugh lunged, peeling chunks out of the leviathan. His hatchet had weakened the flesh of the tentacle, and he struck a savage blow against the nearest beak, splitting the chitinous material beneath. The leviathan roared, and the sound shook the heavens.

Tentacles splayed out and writhed, several of them going taut, revealing the other two beaks and the leviathan's eye. The massive black orb rotated down, flexing and pulsing until it narrowed on Hugh. He lunged with the hatchet again, only to have his arm caught up by a smaller tentacle. Another grasped his left leg, and with a grunt, he realized he was in deep shit.

Hugh meant to call for Alan, but even as the thought crossed his mind, he saw the jet black fur of the other werewolf fending off another Unseelie Fae, keeping it away from Haka as the smaller wolf continued trying to free himself. The leviathan drew him in, ever closer. There were few beings nearby who could face a leviathan, but one might hear his cry.

"Brother of Hinon, bane of Flint, aid us if it is your will!" Hugh's words were caught somewhere between a scream and a howl as the leviathan started to rip the flesh from his legs. But his cry did not go unanswered.

Thunder that threatened to crack open the skies shattered the air around them. Dark clouds boiled across the sky, moving with unnatural speed before the stormfront split. The head of a thunderbird burst forth, the being Hugh had come to know as the Piasa Bird.

Lightning crackled in the bird's eyes, and when it opened its mouth to screech, a storm of lightning blinded them all.

CHAPTER FOURTEEN

V ICKY FROWNED AS the skies ahead of them darkened.

"That's not natural," Luna said, leaning up closer to Vicky as Jasper's wings pulsed beneath them.

"No shit," Vicky said. She patted Jasper's neck. "Find Hugh. We can ask him what the hell is going on."

She felt the trill of Jasper's response beneath her fingers, and the cold air bit into her cheeks as the dragon pushed forward, whipping them through the sky faster.

A few minutes later, the thunderhead cracked open, and lightning roared out of the cloud bank. Vicky stared in shock at the cluster of bolts rocketing to the earth. They were close enough now that the gray clouds dimmed the sun, and they could hear the screams of whatever lay below that storm of lightning. But as fast as the clouds had come, they receded, the lightning stopped, and Vicky saw what looked like the shadow of a massive bird retreat toward the opposite horizon. Below them something roared, and Vicky's heart skipped a beat when they cleared a hill and the flailing tentacles of a leviathan arced into the sky.

Jasper was fast, rolling to the side to avoid one of the hook-covered appendages. But it left Vicky and Luna to do nothing but cling to his back, completely at the mercy of the fight between two titans.

"It has the wolves!" Luna shouted, her voice barely audible over the basso roar of the leviathan.

Vicky understood what the other sounds were now, the high-pitched keening in the vacant armor strewn about the scene below. There had been Fae here, far more than there were now. But she frowned at the form sprinting away below them, its grayish flesh and translucent wings a blur between the branches. Jasper dipped below what she now realized was a blind strike from the leviathan as it attempted to crush everything around it. And it was doing a damn good job. But as they drew lower, Vicky could see the wolves tangled in that rubbery mass of flesh, could see Hugh getting dragged closer to the beak, and that was something she didn't think even a werewolf could survive.

Haka was in no better shape, and neither was the old wolf she assumed was from the Kansas City Pack. They were in trouble, and Vicky's heart ached as she remembered the battle with the Ghost Pack in the Burning Lands. They'd gotten through worse, but they'd also already been dead.

"I'll get you," Vicky shouted. "Get Hugh, Haka, and Alan. The other one looks like he's almost free."

Vicky didn't wait to hear Luna's agreement. She didn't need to. As soon as she spoke the words, the snow-white death bat launched herself off Jasper's back. Before Vicky could so much as light a soulsword, Luna's outstretched wing had already sliced through the tentacle stripping flesh from Haka. The mass thumped to the ground and the leviathan roared, its wet black eye swiveling away from Hugh and focusing on Luna. Vicky knew she wouldn't have a better chance.

"Keep it busy," she shouted to Jasper as she let go. The leviathan had Hugh pinned, one arm against his body, and it looked like it was about to rip his other arm off. That's where Vicky aimed, the thinnest part, and as the foul stench of the leviathan wafted up toward her, the soulsword grew denser, longer, until it met the leviathan's rubbery flesh. Panic rose in Vicky's chest as the tentacle resisted, but it only lasted for a moment. The gray matter of the Abyss creature gave way, and Vicky's soulsword finished its work.

"Get the others!" Hugh grunted. He struck out with

what looked like a stone hatchet, attacking the larger tentacle holding his waist. But the weapon didn't cut like a stone hatchet. It cut deep into the leviathan's flesh. But even so, the blade was small, and it would take many strikes for Hugh to sever the tentacle. Vicky didn't wait. Instead, she lashed out with a soulsword, finishing the cuts that Hugh had started, but as the tentacle fell away, she saw the damage it had done, saw it catch on Hugh's fur, and saw the wall of muscle that poked through Hugh's wounds.

She'd never seen a wolf take that much damage and survive. She gritted her teeth and slashed through the last bit of tentacle holding onto Hugh. The wall started to collapse, but despite his protests, Vicky threw him over her shoulder in a fireman's carry. She sprinted away from the leviathan, behind the old stone ruins, until they were well out of the way of the leviathan's reach before setting him down.

"That's not what I asked you to do," Hugh said, holding a clawed hand to his waist, and Vicky feared he was holding himself together.

"Wait here," Vicky said. "Luna is with me. We'll get the others."

"Keep it away from the Heart," Hugh said.

Vicky's steps faltered as she turned away from the werewolf and Ashley raised a hand in greeting. Vicky gave a quick nod and hurried on. Gaia had sent her here for the Heart. What happened if that thing got to it first? She didn't want to find out. Vicky ran.

✦   ✦   ✦

VICKY SPRINTED BACK toward the thrashing ball of tentacles. The soulsword in her hand brightened, even as the flames licking up around its edges darkened.

Luna managed to carry Haka away as Jasper ripped and scorched the trunk of a larger tentacle.

The Kansas City wolf freed himself, backpedaling and launching another volley of arrows toward the center of the leviathan.

The thunderbird was nowhere to be seen, and while Vicky knew the Piasa Bird was more a force of nature than an ally, she still wished it would return and lend them its strength.

A tentacle shot forward. She barely raised the soulsword in time to split it down the middle. That didn't save her from the inertia. The bleeding gray flesh hit her like a wall. Vicky slammed into the earth, flat on her back, gasping for breath as stars swam across her vision.

She stayed there for a moment, darkness creeping in the periphery of her vision, before she managed to catch enough of her breath to roll out of the way and surge forward once more as the rains slowed.

A white blur leapt to the branches above her before Luna launched herself at Alan. The death bat sliced through another of the leviathan's tentacles, leaving it to writhe on the ground like a dismembered octopus. As fast as they tore it apart, the leviathan healed. Smaller, thinner tentacles struck out at them like whips, cutting through fur and flesh like a razor.

Vicky knew what they needed to do. They needed to get everyone clear so Jasper could do what he did best, but with the injured all around her, that was no small task. Luna squeaked as one of the tentacles managed to backhand her and sent her flailing off into a tree. Vicky closed on the thickest tentacle that had its grip on Alan, hacking at it with her soulsword, squeezing her hand tighter, giving the sword more length, until the last of the flesh gave way with a gristly pop. Alan slumped onto the ground, the black fur of the wolf matted in blood and viscera.

Vicky grabbed him, grunting at the weight of the werewolf. Hugh wasn't exactly light, but Alan felt like she'd put a pallet of bricks on her back, or maybe that was her own injuries catching up with her. It didn't matter now, but Alan's breathing was shallow, and the gurgling wet sounds coming from him told her there was more damage in his chest than there appeared to be. She narrowly avoided one of the newborn tentacles snapping above their head. Vicky awkwardly slashed the thing off with a clumsy strike from the soulsword.

"Jasper!" Vicky snarled. "Burn it!"

Jasper, the normally friendly cuddly dust bunny turned dragon released a roar to equal the leviathan's own. He dove into that squirming ball of death, and the leviathan roared when the dragon's claws found purchase. Vicky wondered what in the hell the dragon was doing, until she remembered the fight they'd had in Nudd's bunker. Jasper could lift the leviathans, and the dragon was smart enough not to unleash the forge-like hell of his flames so close to his friends.

Jasper heaved and roared as tentacles reached up and scraped scales from his body, but it wasn't enough to stop him. The leviathan's tentacles flailed as the dragon gave two mighty flaps of his wings, rolled onto his back, and flung the screeching leviathan over the trees. The impact shook leaves from their perch, and new water fell around them like a fresh rainstorm. Jasper arced up over them, and in the shadows silhouetted by the trees, a bluish streak of hellfire turned the early morning into a surreal landscape. A few seconds later, the piercing cries of the leviathan quieted.

Vicky could've sworn she heard her own heartbeat

in the following silence. She rolled Alan over and grimaced at the massive puncture in his chest. If it was healing, she couldn't see it, which meant he didn't have long.

There were many things she'd learned running with the Ghost Pack, and some of those skills she'd lost since being reborn, but others had remained. So once more, she reached out through the pack bonds. She found the wolves bonded to Hugh, found their injured brethren, and the distant warmth of those who were not. And for a moment, however brief, she thought she could hear the far off cry of the lost necromancer locked away in a reality not his own.

The pack magic flowed through her, changed in her hands, until it became something else, until Alan's ribs snapped, sucked, and crackled their way back to something resembling normalcy. The werewolf's chest changed shape, and he screamed as his eyes shot open a moment before the pain knocked him unconscious once again.

"What are you doing?" Luna asked.

"Trying to save him."

"You're a healer?" she asked.

Vicky grimaced. "I used to be better at it. In the Burning Lands. It's … harder here. It only seems to work with the wolves. Lucky for him."

The Kansas City wolf jumped into the ruins of the stone cabin and hurried toward them. "How is he?"

"Not good," Vicky said. "But I think he's healing himself now."

"You're Vicky. I'm Splitlog." He eyed her and fidgeted a bit. "I'd heard the stories, but I don't know that I believed them."

"She's full of surprises," Haka said, grimacing and sitting down beside Alan. "Did you get my dad out?"

Vicky nodded.

Jasper sailed overhead, circling the area before gliding down, his wings shrinking, and his body slowly returning to the ball of fluff just before he plopped onto Vicky's shoulder. Big black eyes studied Alan and Haka in turn.

"Good job," Vicky said, scratching the dragon between the eyes. "Good job."

CHAPTER FIFTEEN

"WHERE'S MY DAD?" Haka asked.

"I left him by Ashley," Vicky said. "And how bad off is she, by the way?"

Haka shook his head. "We're not sure. The innkeeper is sending a healer. At first, I thought it might be you when you were healing Alan, but if you can only heal the wolves, that won't do Ashley any good."

Luna silently sidled up next to Alan. He was still covered in rich black fur, and she laid a hand on his cheek, the ragged breaths of the werewolf evening out. A small knot untied itself in Vicky's gut.

"You must be Luna," Splitlog said.

Luna looked up at the wolf as he shifted back into his human form. "I am."

Before Splitlog finished his transformation, the wolf was already unpacking a pair of jeans from a backpack at the base of the tree. He slid his narrowing arms into a denim shirt.

Some of the wolves in the River Pack carried their

clothes in a sack tied around their ankle. Vicky wondered if Hugh had been rubbing off on the Kansas City Pack.

Alan started to change. Luna backed away as the massive muscles in his arm flattened, and the fur grew loose and fell to the earth. In a matter of moments, Alan's dark skin showed through the black fur. He looked like a thousand cats had shed on him while he'd been sleeping. The thought made Vicky chuckle.

Alan's eyes fluttered and slowly cracked open. "What the hell happened?"

"Vicky healed you," Luna said. "Also you're still … *quite* naked."

Alan almost jumped to his feet, sending a spray of fur up into the air as his hands shot down to cover his crotch.

"That's really nothing I haven't seen before," Vicky said. "I'm not a kid anymore."

"Kid," Alan said. "I've known you since you were a kid, dammit, and that means you'll always be a kid. When you're ninety damn years old, you'll be a kid. That's how this works. Now turn around so I can get some pants on."

Luna flashed Vicky a toothy grin.

"You too," Alan said.

"Me?" Luna asked, a small whine to her voice as she

teased the werewolf. "I'm not even human."

Alan slowly raised an eyebrow, until they both turned around.

Only Haka remained in wolf form. Perhaps a bit more paranoid than the other two, but Vicky wondered if Haka might be the smartest one in this case.

"Okay," Alan said. "Let's go find Ashley."

Even though Alan had made the suggestion, it was Splitlog who took the lead, heading down the old path in front of the rest of the group.

✦   ✦   ✦

THEY REACHED A small clearing a short time later. Hugh and Ashley waited there, but they weren't alone. Vicky could sense the power near them before she realized what it was, *who* it was. And even as her steps slowed and she held out a hand to stop everyone before they reached Hugh's reclining form, footsteps pounded on the trail ahead. From around the bend, Elizabeth the blood mage appeared, Alexandra at her side.

The tension in Vicky's chest relaxed a fraction. The blood soaking Ashley's chest undid the effect a moment later.

Alexandra looked between Hugh and Ashley. "You did your best to try to die today, didn't you?"

Hugh gave her a pained smile. "Ashley first. The

innkeeper sent you?"

Alexandra nodded. "It would work better if I wasn't alone. I've never been as good at healing as Aideen."

"Better than Foster, though," Hugh said.

Alexandra grinned as she kneeled down next to Ashley. "You better believe it. And feel free to tell him that if you'd like."

It was then Vicky noticed the fresh blood coursing down Elizabeth's arms. The blood mage had cut herself, and recently.

"Your arm," Vicky said.

Elizabeth glanced down and looked up at Vicky as if seeing her for the first time. "It's fine. We needed to find Ashley fast. My stupid phone wouldn't get a signal."

"Used a spell to find her?" Vicky asked.

Elizabeth nodded. "It's simple enough, but I may have cut a little deep in my haste. At least Cornelius isn't here to see it. I'd never hear the end of it."

The blood mages were one of the few magic users that unnerved Vicky. There was a weight in their presence. Something always lurked behind them, or around them. She'd heard the stories of the Shadowlands they summoned creatures from. Vicky had been through a Seal before, lived in the Burning Lands for a time, and she wondered if the Shadowlands were much like that. Or if her experiences in the Abyss, and those other lands, simply made her more sensitive to the blood mages.

Ashley had paled, and Alexandra cursed. She felt around the blade in the priestess's chest. "Damn good thing you didn't pull that out. Sure as hell didn't miss any arteries."

Elizabeth wrung her hands before reaching out and taking Ashley's. "You'll be okay."

Ashley's white lips pulled up into a weak smile before her eyes closed, and she went limp.

Elizabeth reached down to her face, eyes wide. "Ashley? Ashley!"

"This will look bad when I pull the blade out," Alexandra said. "Don't stop me."

Elizabeth nodded, her hands going white as she pulled away and crossed Ashley's beneath her grip.

With one vicious pull, the blade slid out of Ashley's chest. A stream of blood followed it but it didn't spray across the ground. Blood didn't splatter across her friends. Instead, it hung in the air, surrounded by a floating ball of water connected to Alexandra's hand. Even as the knife clattered to the ground, the magic funneled Ashley's blood back into the wound, preventing any further loss.

Alexandra worked like that for a time, and it

seemed like the water floating above Ashley filled with more and more blood, but Vicky stared in awe as Alexandra worked, her form becoming more translucent, pulling the wound wide. She worked in Ashley's chest as if she was a surgeon and this was her operating table.

The arteries slowly came back together, the blood feeding its way back inside of Ashley, until finally the severed artery was whole again, the muscle filaments were carefully laid back down, and a dull white glow ran the length of each cut as Alexandra rebuilt her layer by layer.

This wasn't the bright healing of one of the fairies, this was delicate work, precision. As the last vestige of the wound in Ashley's chest closed, traced by a white line of Alexandra's magic, Ashley gasped.

Elizabeth burst into tears, throwing her arms around Ashley as Alexandra sagged back onto the ground.

"It's done," the water witch said with a deep sigh. "She should recover. She's going to need rest. The blood loss was more than I'd hoped."

"What about Hugh?" Haka asked.

Alexandra smiled. "Why don't you ask him yourself?"

Haka turned and almost stumbled backward.

Hugh was standing there, just finishing up buttoning his shirt. "Just needed some time to heal. I'll be fine. Did you get the Heart?"

"Not yet," Splitlog said. "There were … obstacles. Vicky had to heal Alan's wounds so he didn't keel over."

"We have no time to spare," Hugh said. "Elizabeth, will you take Ashley and Alan back to the lair to rest?"

Elizabeth nodded. "Do you need us?"

"We must keep the Heart safe," Hugh said. "But you must keep our friends safe."

"You don't mind if I … borrow the Heart do you?" Vicky asked.

Hugh started to frown at Vicky, a question on his lips before Elizabeth cut them off.

"This wasn't the only leviathan." She tapped away on her phone. "Look." She turned the phone around, and the slideshow played, showing leviathans in the mountains and rivers. Disgust twisted Hugh's stomach when he saw some of them smashing through residential neighborhoods.

"Nudd," Hugh said.

Elizabeth nodded. "That's what I thought, too. But how in the hell can he do this? Do you remember what it took Ezekiel to summon just one of those things?"

Hugh nodded. "Of course, but how many like Ezekiel labor under the will of Nudd? That I cannot answer."

"Have they only appeared here?" Vicky asked.

Elizabeth turned to Vicky. "Did you see the pictures? They're everywhere."

"That's not what I mean," Vicky said. "What about Faerie?"

Alexandra cursed. "That would be smart of him. If he divided the assault between realms, it would be hard for us to unite in defense."

"What concerns me more is Nudd sent the leviathan here, almost directly on top of the Heart of Quindaro." Hugh turned his gaze to Vicky. "Perhaps he already knows what you seek."

The thought nauseated her. If Nudd knew what she was here for, he might already know what else she needed. She hadn't even talked to Koda yet, didn't know what else she might need to transfer the blood knot.

Luna squeezed her arm. "It's all right, the rest of us are here. We can get the Heart and keep it safe."

"Can we?" Vicky asked, looking up at Luna's dark eyes before turning to Hugh. "Is it safe for me to use it? Do you know why I need it?"

"If the innkeeper sent you here seeking the Heart, I can imagine what you need it for. You mean to transfer the blood knot, so if Damian should die, you will still live."

"Not just me," Vicky said. "Sam too. If any of us die, that's it for all three of us."

"What kind of insane magic are you talking about?" Splitlog asked.

"Old magic," Hugh said. "A magic formed by Ward, binding three souls, and sealed with the blood of the family. It is a nearly unbreakable bond. If death takes one, it takes all three."

Hugh took a deep breath, and his eyes flashed from Luna to Vicky. "What you seek is no small trinket. It is a fragment of a demon, meant to sabotage the people here, that instead brought many together. The risks of carrying it are not small. It can eat away your confidence, raise your paranoia, and force you to question those you would trust the most."

"But can she have it?" Luna asked.

"It is not mine to give," Hugh said. "We may speak of it as an artifact, but it rests in a black altar."

"And how do you expect to get that back?" Ashley asked. "Last person I know who was crazy enough to use one of those was Damian. It brought a demon to his doorstep."

Vicky shrugged. "He still killed it."

Ashley's eyebrows slowly rose as she studied Vicky.

"And he almost died like five times doing it."

Hugh crossed his arms and let out a sigh. "I can take you to the altar, but you'll have to pass the trial yourself if you mean to keep the Heart. I won't stop you from taking it."

"Trial?" Vicky asked. And what at first she thought was tantamount to picking up an antique, she suddenly realized might be far more complicated.

CHAPTER SIXTEEN

ALEXANDRA ACCOMPANIED HUGH, Vicky, and Luna as they returned to the stone cabin. Elizabeth and Splitlog stayed behind to help watch over the others.

"How is Nixie?" Hugh asked.

Alexandra hesitated. "As well as one can expect, I suppose. She's holding herself together."

"And the meeting in the UK?"

"Apparently it went well enough. She's been invited to speak at the UN. She's going, but I wouldn't say she's in the mood for diplomacy. Things are tense among the water witches. Some of Lewena's people returned to the fold, but there are many more who trust no one."

"What was Nixie doing in the UK?" Vicky asked.

Alexandra glanced at her before turning her attention back to the gravel path. "Discussing the state of the war with some of Parliament. Many in the commoners' government there know who she is now. It is a strange thing, to have lived so long in hiding and secrecy, only to have things shift to be so open because of Nudd's war."

"Whether it was Nudd or someone else," Hugh said, "it was always a matter of time."

"I know in some ways you're right," Alexandra said. "But we already threw down the Mad King. And yet here he is once more, still alive, wreaking havoc on a world we thought victorious over him millennia ago."

"Here, now, releasing a leviathan?" Hugh said. "And if he is crazed enough to do that, what else is coming?"

"It means there's some level of desperation in his plans," Alexandra said. "No one can truly control a leviathan. Not even the Mad King."

"He is truly the same Fae?" Hugh asked.

Vicky studied the old wolf. He didn't seem surprised by the revelation, but gods knew most of the others had been. Drake had been right all along. He'd dropped hints, but he'd never come right out and said it. Vicky wondered if it was some old oath he'd made that kept the secrets from his lips and, even if it was, how could that possibly apply to the monster Nudd had become?

"A madman to some," Alexandra said. "And a hero to others. I suppose there will always be some madness in the world, but I do wish they would take a day off."

✦ ✦ ✦

HUGH LED THEM into a circle of barely sunken earth at the center of the stone cabin's ruins.

"The altar is here," Hugh said, gesturing to the ground. "The rest of us can keep watch to make sure the Unseelie Fae do not return, but only one may enter the altar."

"You could always clean up that leviathan," Vicky said. "Smells like burned octopus from here."

Jasper chittered in agreement.

"How do I get in?" Vicky asked.

"It has been almost two centuries since I last saw the altar sink into the ground. I suspect it will rise much the same." He reached out a hand, bent down, and brushed away the earth. Each swipe of his fingers dug into the grass and dirt beneath, until there was something more resistant. Vicky thought she could see a black stone patina peeking through the dirt. Hugh cleared away a little more earth and then placed his palm upon the darkness.

The others stepped back as a series of runes sprang to life, the threat of fiery magic leaping from one to the next, until each, in turn, had been connected by a webwork of knots and runes.

The fires died. And nothing happened.

"The stories of black altars always speak of a blood

price," Hugh said, gripping his hands together. "When dealing with devils, you always pay in blood."

Something clicked in Vicky's memory. The story Damian had once told her. She nodded rapidly. "He's right. Damian wrote a letter in blood and placed it on an altar. Everything has to do with blood with these things."

Hugh sighed and pulled out his phone. He sent a quick text message and brushed more dirt away from the top of the black stone. "I've asked Elizabeth to join us. Offering your blood to demons seldom ends well."

"You think she can get in?" Luna asked. "Without paying the price?"

"No," Hugh said. "But she may be able to tell us something of this magic. There are altars across this world and others. It is best to be cautious."

"But the Heart is hidden inside it?" Vicky asked.

Hugh nodded. "Since the times of the Civil War, when this place was a haven, and many enslaved people found their freedom here. Even Zola's path took her through Quindaro."

Vicky blinked at that, her eyes trailing from the black stone up to Hugh. "Did she hide it? I know she and Philip used to hide shit all over the place."

Hugh chuckled. "That is accurate, but this is not something she hid. This was meant to sabotage the city. To pit nation against nation, and men against men. Instead, it united them. I wish you could have seen this city in those times. There were many good people here, living together in something like harmony, but there was darkness too. I wouldn't trust it to have the same effect in these times."

✦   ✦   ✦

THEY WAITED THERE for a time, until footsteps crunched nearby, and Elizabeth appeared on the path to the stone cabin.

Hugh gestured to the uncovered obsidian disc. He placed his hand on it, calling the fiery runes into existence once more, only to have them fizzle out. "Can you tell how we can get into this? What price it requires?"

Elizabeth frowned at the circle of stone. She pulled her blade from her belt and carved a deep line in her forearm before running her fingers through the blood. Her fingers danced across her skin, drawing patterns and whorls before she splayed her fingers and held them out in front of her. She seemed to be looking through the space between her fingers, studying the earth and something above it no one else could see.

Elizabeth growled. "This is no altar. This is a trap."

"Most of the altars are," Hugh said. "But can you

tell what the price is?"

"The price is blood," Elizabeth said. "But I can see the echoes of what's to come, of who has died in this place before. Whoever activates that altar will likely be trapped inside it." She wrapped gauze around her arm and smeared the blood away from her fingers.

Elizabeth turned her attention back to Hugh. "Whoever goes into that may not be coming out. You activate the altar and a cage is going to close over you. I can see it here." She traced the shape through the air, a kind of rectangle lined up with the angles of the knots tying the runes together. "The depression in the center looks to be the trigger. Put enough blood in it, and there won't be any going back."

"It is the only way to the Heart …" Hugh said, the words trailing away.

But if that was true, and there was no way to save Damian and Sam without it, Vicky didn't have a choice. She pulled on the edge of Luna's wing until it was taut, and sliced deeply into her forearm.

"Hey!" Luna snapped, pulling her wing away.

Before anyone else could so much as protest, before Hugh could grab her and pull her away, the blood coursing down Vicky's arm fell into the depression at the center of the stone. The runes burst into brilliant life, the lines between them turning as bright as the sun before a barrier shimmered into life between her and the others. By the time the divot finished filling with blood, Vicky couldn't see through the glowing walls. Their light dimmed, and a darkness deeper than the Abyss settled all around her.

"Oh no," a deep and brittle voice said. "Little demon, what have you done."

CHAPTER SEVENTEEN

VICKY HADN'T KNOWN what to expect when she stepped onto the altar. But the glowing outline of the horned beast materializing in front of her sure as hell wasn't it. "Who are you?"

"Who am *I*?" the demon asked, baring a row of dagger-like teeth. "I am one who used to be, but is no more."

"Great, riddles." Vicky muttered.

"To take the Heart, you must pass the trial. You can save yourself much pain by dying now instead."

"That's a *great* offer," Vicky said, showing a hard smile. "Why don't we try the trial anyway? Just for fun?"

"Very well." The demon reached out in a flash, and his scaly clawed fingers closed around Vicky's face. In an instant, the darkness vanished, and an old familiar sight rose up in her vision. A vision that couldn't be real, because she left it behind long ago.

But there was no mistaking the old throne room.

No mistaking the plains sweeping out before it, the twisted trees and the trolls who lived within them. This was the Burning Lands.

And even as she thought it, a voice whispered in her mind. *This is where you belong. This is what you are.* And in that moment, her vision turned as if she had stepped outside of her own head, so she could see from outside the throne room, see the figure sitting upon it, the fire in her eyes, the cracked lines running through her flesh, and the corpses below her feet.

Prosperine.

The Destroyer.

Queen of the Burning Lands, the demon who'd had her claws in Vicky for so long, but she was gone now. Vicky had slain her with Damian's help.

Still, she was here, breathing, standing, walking toward Vicky until she reached out a hand and cupped her cheek. "You will never be rid of me, girl. You *are* me."

And for the first time in a very long time, terror crawled down Vicky's spine. It couldn't be real. It wasn't real. She'd overcome this before. Prosperine had killed her friends, slaughtered the werewolves, only to take her over as she rose to power in the Ghost Pack. Prosperine was not her, but the ice crawling into her bones made her want to scream.

"You know what you are," Prosperine said, not breaking eye contact. "I have seen you kill before. How many have you slaughtered now? How many didn't you banish to the Sea of Souls?"

She'd do it again in a heartbeat. Anyone, anything, that came for her friends or family would be struck down. Justice had to be dealt.

"Justice …" Prosperine said with a snide laugh. "You speak of justice, but you are only a murderer. You were born to be the Destroyer, and even after corrupting my power, you still deal in death."

Prosperine leaned in close, baring her teeth. "You enjoy it."

Vicky's heart leapt into her throat at those words. She tried to hide the reaction, the horror of how true those words rang.

"You can't leave me behind, little demon."

Prosperine's face *changed*. The ravaged flesh and blood-red tissue beneath it softened as the chasms drew together, her cheeks filling out until Vicky was staring at someone else. Staring at herself, bloody and hard-eyed with only the faintest traces of the cracked skin of Prosperine.

The scene behind the Destroyer shifted, the darkness becoming a battlefield strewn with the broken bodies of her enemies and the screams of the dying.

But then, as she looked down at the blood pooling into a mirror around her feet, the reflection showed her own face, now savaged with the cracked flesh of the demon, Prosperine.

Her limbs moved, fury rising as if it might seep from the very pores of her skin. This demon was dead, and she'd kill it again, a million times over if that's what it took.

But that was wrong. This was all wrong. Even as the soulsword sprang to life in her hand, she stared into the baleful eyes of the demon, her own eyes, and remembered what Hugh had told her.

"You feed on fear." Vicky drew up to her full height.

"What?"

"You're right," Vicky said, a cold acceptance settling into her chest. "This is a part of me now."

"Every creature in every world has fear, Destroyer. Every. Single. One. And it will destroy you, child. Your kind falls to fear so easily, and it makes you the ideal vessels. You let it twist you by inches until the mirror you look upon shows only evil, but you somehow see justice."

"It's part of me." Vicky felt shaky as she stepped away from the demon. "I see it now, thanks to you. I can hold it back. I can fight it, fight me." Vicky let the soulsword snap out of existence.

The demon cocked its head to the side. The curiosity on its face turned to something else. Turned to anger, with a fleck of the demon's own fear. "Strike me down as you were meant to do!"

"No." Vicky stood in the silent darkness, the hiss from the demon the only sound in the world. "I see you."

And with those words, Vicky's twisted reflection and the field of dead vanished, leaving her in darkness. The shadows around her brightened into a dim golden glow, as if the Abyss itself was waiting just outside that room.

"I don't understand," the demon wailed. "You, of all creatures…"

"Where is your Heart?" Vicky asked.

There was a hesitation in the dim light before the voice spoke again, and Vicky could hear the resignation behind it. "The Heart is not here. It is buried beneath the old tree in the cemetery. The one they call the Signal Tree. Now go. Leave me to rot in this prison."

"Who are you?"

The demon, now diminutive, fragile-looking, turned away on his goat-like legs. "I have had many names. Some would rot your tongue from your mouth.

The commoners called me Agramon."

For a moment, Vicky wondered how she could get back out of the altar. Then Agramon traced a symbol in the air. A twisted rune that looked something like Uruz. Fire erupted across her body. The darkness vanished, and the circle of stone smoked beneath her feet.

Vicky looked up to Hugh and said, "We have to get to the Signal Tree."

"You're alive," Hugh said.

"Geez, give me some credit," Vicky muttered, giving Hugh a shaky grin.

"We could hear you talking in the altar," Hugh said, a crease forming in his brow.

"It was more like mumbling," Luna said. "We couldn't actually hear any words."

Vicky tried not to make it too obvious how much relief she felt at Luna's words. She didn't want them to know about those secret fears. No one need ever know.

"Then I guess we better be off to the Signal Tree," Elizabeth said, prodding at the gauze on her wrist.

"Are you sure you don't wish to stay with Ashley?" Hugh asked.

Elizabeth closed her eyes for a moment before answering. "No. Better safe than sorry. You could use a hand if you run into any more of those Unseelie Fae."

Jasper trilled on Luna's shoulder.

"That's right," Vicky said. "You can have more crunchy snacks."

"What did you see?" Hugh asked.

"I think it was the demon," Vicky said as Hugh started down the path that would take them toward the old cemetery. It twisted around, until he reached a hill. "But at the end, when he lost, he looked small. Like he knew he was defeated."

Hugh nodded. "The stories say you face your own demons inside the Heart."

Vicky didn't respond.

"You don't have to tell me what you saw, but know that it was both true, and not. You have the strength to change your fate. Everyone does, but some do not realize it. As for the demon himself, he fell long ago, and his purpose inside the Heart failed as well."

Hugh's words rang true, but Vicky didn't want to tell him about what she'd seen. She'd looked into the face of the Destroyer once more, and it had been her own.

They crossed out of the woods and onto the gravel close to the river before turning back toward the hills. "Sometimes I forget how beautiful it is here," Elizabeth said.

"Only because you are insensitive to the dead,"

Luna said, rubbing her arms as if she was freezing.

"What are you, some kind of bat necromancer?" Elizabeth asked.

Luna laughed. "I've never heard it put like that before. The death bats are just sensitive to ghosts. And there are a lot around here."

"This is a place of much loss." Hugh glanced back at them before turning his attention to the woods. He crossed the path, and they started up hill once more. "The river crossing behind us is where many slaves escaped Missouri."

"Why so many ghosts then?" Luna asked.

"Because many of those slaves died here," Hugh said. "Slave catchers and disease caught up with some of them. Others were too weak, too malnourished to survive the trip across the frozen rivers. Many of them are buried here. It is a solemn place, and one that has its fair share of ghosts."

"Why did the town die?" Vicky asked.

Hugh frowned. "It did not die, exactly. Many moved on as Kansas City grew up around it. The Heart's misguided influence could only reach so far. In time, men not under the power of the Heart set this town on a path to what you see today." Hugh glanced back toward the more modern parts of Quindaro. "I am glad something of it remains."

They climbed in silence for a time, until the group crested the hill, and the cemetery lay sprawled out in front of them. Modest tombstones peppered the area with grass flattened by more traffic than Vicky would have expected to see there.

She didn't have to ask which tree was the Signal Tree. There was no doubt in her mind when she saw the bare branches, forked and reaching to the heavens. A massive trunk split into three huge arms, all nearly vertical.

"That's it?" Elizabeth asked.

"It is," Hugh said.

Vicky walked around the trunk, frowning at the earth. There weren't any obvious sunken areas, nothing like the disc that had led to the altar. "I don't see anything."

"How much has that tree grown since it was buried here?" Elizabeth asked. "It could've been swallowed by the root ball."

"It may have been swallowed," Hugh said, a small smile edging its way across his lips. "And all the times I visited this place, I never realized what was here. Tell the Signal Tree who you met."

"What do you mean?" Vicky asked.

Luna's ears perked up, and the snow-white death bat almost bounced on the balls of her feet. "Stump, or

Dirge, or Appalachia!"

Vicky's gaze snapped back to Hugh and slowly focused on the Signal Tree. She laid her hand on one of the branches and said simply, "Appalachia sent me. By way of Dirge, and their friend the green man known as Stump. I've journeyed far, and spoke to the demon in the altar. I seek the Heart."

The bark split beneath her fingers but Vicky didn't pull away. She watched as a thin line of sap dripped from the wound, the wound widening as the trunk cracked and the ground roiled at her feet. A lump shifted beneath the bark, as if a knot on the tree was traveling from the roots into the wound in the old branch. And there, as Vicky watched, a small stone not much larger than a quarter oozed its way out of the tree. She plucked it from the sap, and realized with a start it was a fragment of a horn. A fragment of the demon's horn, imbued with a power that had become the Heart of Quindaro.

Luna ran her hand across the old tree. "Thank you."

Vicky knew it wasn't just a tree, but it didn't seem to be a green man either. "What is this tree?"

"An old Forest God," Hugh said. "Many of the trees here are gone now. I suppose there are yet enough she still stands sentinel. And for that we must thank her."

CHAPTER EIGHTEEN

ELIZABETH HURRIED AHEAD while Hugh led the group back to the lair beneath the old brewery. It was an odd thing to see the Heart retrieved. It was artifact he knew existed, but he had been mistaken about its location for many years. He wondered if it had been moved, or if it had simply never been placed in the altar. But the stories around the Heart were many, and he wasn't entirely surprised some parts of the stories were wrong.

One story told of a necromancer working with what would become the Confederacy who planted the Heart. Missouri had always been a battleground in those times, and there were men, and fouler things, who would not have hesitated to stoop to sabotage. Zola and Philip weren't the only necromancers who stained their hands with blood in that war.

The grounds around the lair weren't as damaged as Hugh had feared. The flying heads had certainly toppled a few stones, and created deep divots in the earth, but the structure was sound. He hunched over, leading the way through the tunnel until he could open the steel door at the end. They'd been lucky today. None of them had succumbed to the leviathan, and Vicky had been successful entering the altar. But the arrival of the Unseelie Fae made Hugh uneasy. It was a new variable he hadn't seen coming.

Inside the lair, Hugh breathed a sigh of relief. Elizabeth and Ashley were curled up on the couch beneath an old blanket. Ashley still looked pale, but Elizabeth greeted them with a smile, carefully edging away from Ashley so as to not wake her up.

"How is she?" Hugh asked.

"Good," Elizabeth said. "Alexandra is better at these things than she'd ever admit to."

"Many of the water witches are," Hugh said. "But you've been friends with her longer than most."

Elizabeth nodded. "I was practically a kid."

"The undines have been formidable enemies over the years, but I am happy they have become stalwart allies."

"Leave it to Damian," Vicky said as she shuffled past Hugh and plopped down on the couch beside Ashley. Her fingers blurred across her phone as she muttered to herself.

Luna stretched her wings before she settled in next

to Vicky, pulling out her own phone and squinting at the screen. "That's not good. Cizin texted me."

"Your overly paranoid babysitter?" Vicky asked. "I'm sure he'll recover."

Luna huffed. "If you hadn't ignored him last time, this wouldn't be an issue."

"Look, you wanted me to play your gym battle. I did. I never would've heard the end of it if your Blastoise had gotten knocked out. I'm not a poké-mancer."

Luna pounded out a message back to Cizin and grinned at Vicky. "Like you said, he'll get over it."

"Have you heard from anyone else?" Hugh asked.

Elizabeth shook her head. "Twitter's on fire with Eldritch sightings. It's not good."

"Where else have they hit?"

"Everywhere," Elizabeth said, her voice quiet. "Some of them make perfect sense. One not far from Antietam. I suspect his target was the Irish Brigade. Others are in major cities."

Hugh let out a slow breath. "Then we may need Camazotz sooner than we thought. I hope he'll be well-rested by nightfall."

"Splitlog, Alan, and Haka?" Luna asked.

"They're resting," Elizabeth said. "Alan tells me they transformed more than once. Exhausting in itself, and with those injuries, I'm not surprised they're done."

"They deserve the rest." Hugh's own wounds nagged at him. He could heal fast, but some of the deeper damage took more time. It was easy to put on a strong presentation, present a strong face to the world, but that didn't mean he wasn't hurt. A day's rest and he might be ready to fight again. But bone-deep exhaustion settled over him like a weight.

"I have to get to Coldwater," Vicky said, looking up from her phone. "Zola just texted to say she got the trunk out of Death's Door." She paused and frowned.

Vicky cursed under her breath. "She says we might need more relics than we thought. Apparently, she found something in one of Damian's manuscripts."

"You best be on your way to Coldwater. Don't want to keep Zola waiting."

Vicky stared at the Heart of Quindaro in her hand. "What will you do now?"

"I'll need to hunt down those flying heads. They need to be imprisoned before they can do more harm." Hugh wrung his hands together and frowned. "Be cautious while the Heart is with you. If you feel rage and anger that is unusual, remember the Heart can have influence over you. Its purpose may have failed here in Quindaro, but it is still a potent artifact. And you would do best to be cautious."

Vicky nodded. "We will." She turned to Luna. "You're coming with me, right?"

Jasper chittered on Luna's shoulder.

"Doesn't sound like he's giving me much of a choice," Luna said, scratching the dragon between its furball eyes.

Hugh thought it would be best if they checked in with Camazotz before Luna left once more with Vicky, but on the same token, Camazotz was going to need as much rest as he could get. So instead he gave each of the girls a hug in turn, remembering how small Vicky had been when he first met her ghost. And now this young woman of flesh and bone might be one of their greatest hopes without Damian. But that was a fact she need not know. The weight of such knowledge could do more damage than the trials that came with it.

✦   ✦   ✦

ONCE THE OTHER wolves were sleeping in one room, while Ashley and Elizabeth took the other, Hugh found himself staring at his phone, sitting on the wide sectional couch in the main room of the lair. He took a deep breath, closed his eyes for a moment, and called the other side of the world.

It rang four times, and he was about to hang up

and send a text when static cracked across the line, and a familiar voice said "Hugh?"

"Euphemia," Hugh said. "How is Nixie?"

Euphemia let out a humorless laugh. "How is our queen?" Her voice was barely a whisper. "The presentations to Parliament in the UK went relatively well, and they were appreciative of us telling them how to murder our kind."

"Euphemia …" Hugh started.

"I get it," Euphemia said. "I understand why it had to be done. It doesn't mean I have to like it."

"But she's okay?" Hugh asked. "The ceremony is done? She's been given the artifacts that come with her station?"

"Yes," Euphemia said. "I'm not entirely sure if that's actually helped anything."

Euphemia paused for a moment. "But to the core of your question, no, she's not okay. She's shown a level of coldness I've not seen from her in a very long time. She's ready to kill, Hugh, and everyone knows it. Some of her own people have shown some reticence around her. People who should have nothing to fear from her."

"And what of Lewena's people?"

"Some have joined us. Others fled, but the witches fear her. That is one good thing to come of this business. They are certainly not what concerns me at the moment."

Hugh nodded to himself. "Tell Nixie that Vicky came for the Heart of Quindaro. She has it now, and I expect she's going to need much more in her gambit. And Euphemia?"

"Yes?"

"Do you remember the story I once told you of the evil spirits who live in waterfalls and wait to drown people? It is said Flint himself placed them in the waters even as he forced the rivers to always flow in one direction."

"It's a hard story to forget, Hugh. Even after all these years."

"The story isn't about any of you. It never was. Please tell Nixie that. Remind her she is better than the darker spirits."

Euphemia was silent for a time. "She's powerful, Hugh. And now … what can she do with that kind of power?"

"The only thing I hope she can do is save herself," Hugh said.

CHAPTER NINETEEN

EUPHEMIA HUNG UP the phone and pinched the bridge of her nose. One more complication. There was always another complication. And that wasn't something she, or any of their allies needed.

She paced the stone hallway. She didn't like that Nixie had gone alone to speak with an auditorium of politicians. The commoners could be as deceitful as Nudd himself, and worse than that, tactless and ignorant. And if Euphemia's patience with the commoners was thinning, she knew Nixie's was gone.

✦   ✦   ✦

"AND HOW MISS ... Nixie is it?" the diminutive man in a finely cut suit asked. He didn't wait for her to answer, instead tapping his pen on a legal pad and continuing. "How can we trust *anything* your people have to say? You've promised peace, but now one of your own kind has nuclear weapons at their disposal."

"Minister," Nixie said, reining in her irritation. "I

have given you my truth. Do with it what you will. I do not believe you are at risk of having those weapons turned on you because the Fae in question wish to live in your world. It would do them no good to implement a 'scorched earth' policy as there are no assurances while Nudd still holds your weapons."

"My colleagues from the UK seem to agree with you," the man said, "but I see little to no reason for that. It seems this man, this self-proclaimed king, has weapons we can scarcely comprehend. And you ask us to simply *trust* you?"

"Gwynn Ap Nudd represents only a fraction of the people from our lands, from Faerie. Most wish only to live in peace with the commoners, though in peace with less pollution would be appreciated." She almost bit her tongue at the slip. "But yes, most of us wish for peace, but as your own alliances are, we are also prepared for war."

"With us?" the minister asked.

"No, Minister. As I said before, we have no desire for a war with the commoners, with humanity. Gwynn Ap Nudd has been a thorn in the side of the Faerie communities for far too long. We wish to bring his reign to an end. It is with that in mind I ask you to let us end this war on our own terms. Your forces are not equipped to face Nudd in open battle, and we cannot let our focus stray."

"There are creatures walking the earth the likes of which we've never seen," said a translator in a bright blue jacket. "If these leviathans, as you've called them, appear near cities, we will have no choice but to engage them."

Another speaker picked up. "And is it such a bad thing that we won't have nuclear capabilities to drop on our own soil? I think not. Conventional weapons can clearly damage those creatures."

"Silence, please," the minister said, tapping his pen on the legal pad once more. "You've given us valuable information here today, and it won't be forgotten. But you understand why we can't trust in all you say?"

"I've given you information to slay my kind," Nixie said. "There is no greater trust one can offer."

The minister frowned. To some degree, Nixie now understood the commoners' comprehension only went so far. They'd become so proficient at killing each other that simply revealing the way in which one might be killed was nothing to them. It was just one more blade in a killing machine.

"We will take your words under advisement. Thank you again for your time today."

Nixie nodded and studied the mostly empty chamber as she left. Towering golden curtains and paintings stretched from floor to ceiling, crowned by a balcony high above. She departed in silence, exiting the building and following the path to a pond with a bronze sculpture in the center. It looked something like a globe, but formed of men and creatures. Nixie didn't pay it much mind as she slipped into the stagnant water and vanished into the cracks below.

She could have walked to the river, but this would be faster. The smell certainly wasn't better, but soon enough, she reached freedom and rocketed through the waters.

✦   ✦   ✦

EUPHEMIA HADN'T BEEN waiting long when the latch clicked open on a massive marble door at the end of the hall. A crack widened in the center between two doors, and Nixie slipped through. The crown sitting on her head gleamed almost as much as the water woven into the braid of hair beneath it. It was a subtle magic, but enough to have impressed upon the commoners she wasn't one of them.

"My Queen," Euphemia said. "All goes well?"

Nixie eyed Euphemia and stalked toward her. She paused at the foot of the stairs that led up to the ornamental throne, a far cry from the seat the water witches actually held in regard of royalty. This was more like something Nudd would prefer, gaudy and without purpose other than to make those around it feel small.

"Come," Nixie said, and led the way behind the throne.

Euphemia followed her into the narrow passage. If one didn't know there was another room hidden behind the textured wall, it would have been nearly impossible to detect.

Nixie deftly touched a faded pattern of runes before swiping a perfectly vertical line through the now-illuminated ward with her index finger.

Gears clicked and hissed in the door, and the textured wall ground in its tracks, revealing a space large enough for the water witches to easily slip through.

Euphemia took a deep breath and followed.

✦   ✦   ✦

NIXIE STARED AT the far table of artifacts resting in the throne room. She'd always known the stories, the rumors that when a queen took over, she'd inherit the relics of the forgotten ages. But this was beyond what she'd imagined. It would take months, if not years, to understand everything that waited in that hidden chamber.

Some things she'd recognized—legendary blades imbued with the power of the stone daggers, circlets, and bracelets that held soulstones of twisted abilities and could give strength beyond imagining. But other things she was unfamiliar with. In fact, all of her allies were. An old clock, something that looked like it would have been at home with the Antikythera shipwreck, a pile of shattered stones with runes etched into them, old bronze armor, and far more bizarre items graced the hall.

But there was only one thing Nixie was focused on now: the ancient gauntlet, tarnished with rigid joints until she slid it over her hand. Then, despite the worst of the wear, the gauntlet moved as silently as if it were her own flesh.

The door clicked closed behind Euphemia as stone met stone once more.

"Zola texted me as I was leaving the UN," Nixie said, pulling a thin disc out of a pouch in her silver armor and leaning over the basin of water in the floor.

"Are you sure the Wasser-Münzen is safe?" Euphemia asked.

"I trust it more than the phone I had among those commoners," Nixie said. "I don't know much about their spying technology, but Damian has told me enough."

They waited for a few short minutes before the disc pulsed and brightened. Whorls moved through the water, and it wasn't long before another voice joined them in the chamber.

"Girl," Zola rasped, her face forming in the basin of water. "If this wasn't important, Ah'd be mighty annoyed. Ah'm standing in a *pond* right now."

Nixie nodded at the old Cajun. "It is good to see you, my friend."

Zola grunted in something like agreement. "Your meeting went well?"

"Relatively. But let me say I think it's fortunate all of the countries in that room have lost access to their nuclear bombs."

"Ah don't doubt that. Ah don't doubt that one bit. But it's not *all* their bombs they've lost access to."

"I know."

"Did you convince them it was you who stopped Damian's rampage?"

Just hearing his name sent a pang of loss through Nixie's chest, and her teeth gnashed together before a flash of rage burned it away. "I did. They have no reason to believe otherwise."

Zola's image blurred as she inclined her head. "Good, good. Commoners who believe you've sacrificed something to save them are far more likely to listen to reason."

"Why?" Euphemia asked, stepping closer to the basin.

Zola squinted. "Trust. Ah suppose that's something you don't have to deal with in your culture."

"I would have agreed with you ten years ago," Euphemia said. "But times have changed a great deal.

Regardless, I have to tell you both what Hugh told me."

"Vicky has the Heart," Zola said.

"Y-yes," Euphemia said.

Zola nodded.

"Vicky was in Quindaro?" Nixie asked with a frown. "Why?"

"For the Heart," Euphemia said.

"Tell her the rest after we hang up this damn water phone," Zola said.

"Water phone?" Euphemia asked.

Nixie grinned at the grumpy Cajun.

"Don't go smiling just yet," Zola said. "Ah'm afraid if we mean to save Damian, we're going to need the Eye of Atlantis."

Nixie froze. "How do you even know about the Eye?"

"An old ghost who knows more than he should."

Koda, Nixie figured. If anyone knew as much about the lost city as the undines, it would be Koda and the Society of Flame. She nodded to Zola. "If that's what it takes."

"That's not all it will take. Euphemia can fill you in on the rest, assuming Hugh told her."

"He did."

"Good," Zola said. "Then find the Eye, or we might lose all three of them anyway. This war has more than

135

two sides. Ah hope you both can see that. Nudd has unleashed the Eldritch on the commoners. Ah don't know if we can stop him." She looked away for a time before turning back to Nixie and Euphemia. "If this goes bad, we're going to lose more than our friends."

Zola's image flickered and faded, and Nixie knew the old Cajun had broken the connection with the Wasser-Münzen. Nixie pulled her own disc out of the basin and slid it back into a pouch in her armor.

"What happened in Quindaro?"

So Euphemia told her of the Heart, the leviathan, and the monsters not seen around Kansas City in centuries. Dark things were walking the world of the commoners once more, and it was going to take a war to stop the machinations of the Mad King. The Eldritch things had appeared in more places than just those she'd heard about. It wasn't good, but it might not be all bad.

Nixie stood stock still for a moment, her lips quivering for the blink of an eye before her stony façade settled into place again. "Then we have hope. We might be able to save all three of them."

"It's possible," Euphemia said, "but at what cost?"

Nixie ran her fingertips over the back of the gauntlet on her right hand. "At any cost."

"My Queen," Euphemia said, hand on her heart as she bowed slightly to Nixie.

✦ ✦ ✦

NIXIE AND EUPHEMIA pored over the tanned maps of their old home.

"I haven't been back in over a century," Nixie said, tapping the outer ring of Atlantis.

"A century?" Euphemia asked. "I haven't been since it sank into the ocean."

"I returned once, after the commoners' Civil War ended. You know I always liked the forts at Old San Juan. The architecture always reminded me of the fortifications that once stood at the edges of Atlantis."

"Was there much left?"

"Deep in the trench there was. But so close to the bottom there are a great many things that pose a danger."

"If Zola knows about the Eye, and Nudd sent a leviathan to destroy the Heart of Quindaro, do you think he knows what we're after?"

"Or he sent a leviathan to keep them from the Heart. Either way, it wouldn't surprise me. He has to know it was one of us who took Damian into the Abyss. Gaia can't act on her own, trapped as she is by Nudd's compulsion."

Euphemia cracked a humorless smile. "Glad to see something backfired on the bastard. But don't you think it's possible he sent something to seek out the

Eye of Atlantis too?"

Nixie nodded. "I'd say it's probable if the Eye survived the collapse of the city. I need to get into the ruins."

"You need to speak to the undines, Nixie. They're restless, and Lewena's factions are still a threat."

"I know."

"Nixie—"

"I will handle them, Euphemia."

Euphemia paused for a time. "My queen, don't become the thing your people fear."

Nixie knew Euphemia meant well, but she still bristled at the words. She nodded, hoping that would bring an end to the undine's commentary for the time being. "Watch over things while I'm gone." She ran a finger down the back of the gauntlet, bringing to life a webwork of golden runes.

"It's not wise to walk the Abyss alone," Euphemia said.

Nixie didn't respond. Her fingers flowed across the gauntlet as if it was a pattern she'd always known, instead of one that seemed to have come to her when she took the throne. The warm glow of the hidden room faded, replaced by darkness and a momentary feeling of weightlessness. Nixie's feet slammed down onto something solid, and a dim golden path stretched out before her in the blackness of the Abyss.

CHAPTER TWENTY

THE ABYSS HAD always been a kind of forbidden place to the water witches, the center of many a story that served to warn even the most curious of them away. But every time Nixie set foot in it, she felt she had stepped past the bounds of the beliefs of the undines. There was something liberating there in the darkness, a chaos that lived and breathed outside her reality.

The first time she'd come here alone she was surprised to find herself walking on the same sort of path that had appeared when she'd been here with Gaia and Damian. Nixie had been in the Abyss before, long ago, but there had been no path to tread upon then. There had been only an empty darkness to fall through, until some creature or power ripped you out of it. Nixie glanced down at the gauntlet on her hand, its runes still glowing with golden light that was soon matched by the stars of the Abyss in the distance.

Her pace quickened, even as she eyed the monstrosities around her with some fascination. A few were simply leviathans—creatures familiar to the undines—deep dwellers who were known to savage ships and sailors alike. In that way, they were not so unlike the undines of old. But things were changing, the witches were changing, and it was in no small part thanks to Damian.

Nixie's steps slowed as she passed a behemoth formed of nothing but eyeballs. Random orbs blinked lids that seem to retract fully behind them in slow motion. The pattern was mesmerizing, but Nixie had no clue what the thing was, or what danger it posed. But if there was one thing she understood about the Abyss, it was the simple fact everything here posed a danger. Even if you couldn't see it at first, danger was there. Seeing those things made her wonder what she'd find when she caught up with Damian. How much time did he have left?

She left the towering multi-eyed creature behind, until she reached something she had never seen before, a fork in the golden path. When she'd been here with Gaia, and when she'd come alone, it hadn't been there. Most of these creatures hadn't been there either.

At the center of the crossroads sat of bizarre, gro-tesque vision. It was madness to look upon, random arms and legs and screaming mouths set into what appeared to be no more than a bulbous gray mass. But it was so littered with appendages, so coated in chaos, Nixie felt unsettled looking at it. But why here? Why was there a crossroads, a fork?

She couldn't ponder the fact that long. The horrid cloud inched ever closer, and slowed as it was, the mass grew visibly larger. Without time to choose, she turned to the left. A moment before Nixie stepped onto that path, a voice echoed around her. "Not there. Never there."

Nixie froze. Some of the golden stars floated down toward her, settling onto the outline of an ethereal woman glowing in gold.

"Gaia?" Nixie said. Gaia had been bound here by the Mad King, so why would she appear now? She responded to Damian, and it made some sense Vicky had been able to communicate with Gaia as she too was bound to him. But Nixie had no such tie. Gaia could as easily strike her down as offer her insight into which fork to take.

"I mean you no harm," Gaia said, as if she'd read the thought from Nixie's mind. "You are bonded to my master, and I am certain he would not see you harmed."

Nixie frowned. "That sounds dangerously close to free will. Not that I would complain about any assistance you have to offer."

Gaia inclined her head. "The right will lead you to Damian. The left to madness."

Nixie didn't have much reason not to trust Gaia. A Titan though she might have been, she was very much like an Old God, and Old Gods could be tricky on their best days. But Nixie had the gauntlet. She could flee from the Abyss with the stroke of one finger. That measure of safety, though it might not be enough to save her, bolstered her choice. She stepped to the right, and almost immediately the gray cloud of limbs and teeth and tongues vanished.

"You've heard the plan from Damian?" Gaia asked.

Nixie narrowed her eyes at Gaia. "I don't understand what you mean. I haven't heard anything from Damian."

"From his extension. His soul."

Then it clicked in Nixie's mind. "You mean Vicky. Zola told me what they need. To transfer the blood knot? Do you think it will be enough?"

"Not on its own," Gaia said.

"The Eye of Atlantis," Nixie said.

"Yes. And are you ready to return to the places of your past? To face what trials may await you there?"

Nixie looked to the distance, nothing around them but blackness and pinpricks of golden light. "Is anyone ever really ready to go home?"

Gaia didn't answer. Instead, she looked up at the towering shadow that suddenly appeared to the right of the path. Pressure threatened the back of Nixie's eyes as she stared up at Damian's form, clad in the mantle of Anubis. He once told her the reason Ezekiel's form had been so grotesque, so fractured, was because he was not the true mantle bearer.

But now Damian was shot through with that same corruption. Something had changed. Whatever had happened to him in Falias had altered the mantle once more. The stories of Anubis said the god would judge the weight of a man's heart against a feather. Perhaps in the joining of Hern that judgment had a poor outcome. Perhaps Anubis still judged men's hearts, and had found the darkness inside.

The jackal-like mouth cracked open, fissures racing across the corners of the giant mouth. A black tongue sat inside, and the pressure of sadness behind Nixie's eyes dried up in a rising fury.

"I'll get you out of this," Nixie said between gritted teeth. "I'll get you out of this or we'll all drown together."

"Then you know what you must do," Gaia said.

"You know what I seek in Atlantis?" Nixie asked. "You understand what it is? What it can do?"

Gaia inclined her head. "The Eye has existed far longer than Atlantis did. Return to your city that once was, so the fate of our friend may at last be decided."

Nixie turned back to Damian. To the monster he'd become. "I love you." She ran two fingers across the back of the gauntlet, and in a heartbeat, the Abyss vanished around her.

Note from Eric R. Asher

Thank you for spending time with the misfits! I'm blown away by the fantastic reader response to this series, and am so grateful to you all. The next book of misadventures is called *The Book of the Sea*, and it's available soon (or maybe now because I'm lazy about updating these things).

If you'd like an email when each new book releases, sign up for my mailing list (www.ericrasher.com). Emails only go out about once per month and your information is closely guarded by hungry cu siths.

Also, follow me on BookBub (book-bub.com/authors/eric-r-asher), and you'll always get an email for special sales.

Thanks for reading!
Eric

The Book of the Sea

The Vesik Series, book #11

By Eric R. Asher

Also by Eric R. Asher

Keep track of Eric's new releases by receiving an email on release day. It's fast and easy to sign up for Eric's mailing list, and you'll also get an ebook copy of the subscriber exclusive anthology, *Whispers of War*.

Go here to get started: www.ericrasher.com

The Steamborn Trilogy:

Steamborn

Steamforged

Steamsworn

The Vesik Series:

(Recommended for Ages 17+)

Days Gone Bad

Wolves and the River of Stone

Winter's Demon

This Broken World

Destroyer Rising

Rattle the Bones

Witch Queen's War

Forgotten Ghosts

The Book of the Ghost

The Book of the Claw*

The Book of the Sea*

The Book of the Staff*
The Book of the Rune*
The Book of the Sails*
The Book of the Wing*
The Book of the Blade*
The Book of the Fang*
The Book of the Reaper*

The Vesik Series Box Sets

Box Set One (Books 1-3)
Box Set Two (Books 4-6)
Box Set Three (Books 7-8)
Box Set Four: The Books of the Dead Part 1 (Coming in 2020)*
Box Set Five: The Books of the Dead Part 2 (Coming in 2020)*

Mason Dixon – Monster Hunter:

Episode One
Episode Two
Episode Three

*Want to receive an email when one of Eric's books releases? Sign up for Eric's mailing list.
www.ericrasher.com

About the Author

Eric is a former bookseller, cellist, and comic seller currently living in Saint Louis, Missouri. A lifelong enthusiast of books, music, toys, and games, he discovered a love for the written word after being dragged to the library by his parents at a young age. When he is not writing, you can usually find him reading, gaming, or buried beneath a small avalanche of Transformers. For more about Eric, see: www.ericrasher.com

Enjoy this book? You can make a big difference.

Reviews are the most powerful tools I have when it comes to getting attention for my books. I don't have a huge marketing budget like some New York publishers, but I have something even better.

A committed and loyal bunch of readers.

Honest reviews help bring my books to the attention of other readers.

If you've enjoyed this book, I would be very grateful if you could take a minute to leave a review. It can be as short as you like. Thank you for spending time with Damian and the misfits.

Connect with Eric R. Asher Online:

Twitter: @ericrasher

Instagram: @ericrasher

Facebook: EricRAsher

www.ericrasher.com

eric@ericrasher.com

Made in the USA
Monee, IL
27 March 2023